Nigel Tourneur

Hidden Witchery

Nigel Tourneur

Hidden Witchery

ISBN/EAN: 9783337388522

Printed in Europe, USA, Canada, Australia, Japan

Cover: Foto ©Andreas Hilbeck / pixelio.de

More available books at **www.hansebooks.com**

HIDDEN WITCHERY.
BY NIGEL TOURNEUR.

DECORATED
BY
WILL MEIN.

LONDON:
LEONARD SMITHERS.
MDCCCXCVIII.

To

ONE EVER KIND,

Whose gracious personality and tender interest in a captious invalid have made bitter-life sweet, and dark malignant hours of sickness and doubt and care fleeting as the sunny moments of a gay April morn:

THIS TENTATIVE LITTLE BOOK.

ADVERTISEMENT.

. . . Till irremeable Old Age sets his knotted hands to the shafts, Passion wheels the vehicle of Life; sometimes visibly, sometimes invisibly. . . . Throughout the following stories and sketches—scantily in part, and, it is feared, obscurely, through symbolism— there may be traced the inception, growth, strength, waywardness, and maturity of its physical manhood, culminating in self-knowledge and abnegation. . . .

N. T.

London, Shrovetide, 1898.

CONTENTS.

THE APOGÆON OF CUPID.

B

THE APOGÆON OF CUPID.

I.

NONE had ever observed her—of this I was certain. I had heard no one talk of her, and I hugged my felicity to me.

When the mavis and blackbird lavished their ringing notes upon the soft spring air, and heavy boughs of peach and cherry scattered fragrant blossoms upon the young green grass, it was then, that, in the dim portals of the woods she importuned alluringly my panting soul.

Indeed, she had invaded my eyes with the silent armies of her beauty ; rendering me a pitiful victim to the unbounded longings of my heart.

By Dian's fountain she was wont to loiter. There, ensconced behind a leafy sheet of clinging ivy that veiled the entrance to the grot, she would linger through the short spring hours; drinking in the balmy scents, listening to the woodland song around her.

Often, when I, passing that way, drank of the bubbling water that fell from the satyr's head, I could declare her eyes were upon me. Nay, had I not twice discovered her, when the seals of slumber had fastened upon her eyelids? and closer attention had but rivetted my heart the firmer to her. What man could withstand her beauty? Certes! when I surprised her one afternoon lying aslumber upon a bench, the picture had transfixed my senses, and I stood all agape as a most veritable Cymon.

This fountain was of old-time fashioning, and age had embellished its artistry. From it the glades lead in all directions; thither came deer to drink, and all sorts of birds to build about and bath in it.

Ofttimes approaching quietly, I would come upon birdkind perched upon the curling snakes that wreathed about the massive basin, all a-busy pruning and dressing their dainty plumes ; so, from frequent sight they closed an acquaintance, even to perching upon my outstretched hand.

Many times had they seen her. Nay, did they not see my lady every hour she was abroad, for whence their amorous twitterings and play. Only her presence could bestow such joys.

Sometimes, as I lay deep in the wind-blown grasses, weaving idle rhymes and lending an ear to the many murmurs in the air, it was, as she were nigh. Then my eager heart leapt up to encounter the steady gaze of her starlike eyes : yet alas, she would pass into another glade.

Never durst I follow. Fear of her exceeding displeasure dispelled all courage ; so, cowing under the dread of her rebuke, I would remain awaiting her return.

At times a formed resolve possessed me : boldly would I accost her, and, pleading my love, risk all denial. But thought of her countenance hardening into disdain dissolved determination ; and that, notwithstanding the lashing cords of love.

II.

"You have seen her then" he cried, and peered amusedly at me. "I had thought as much:" and laughing softly to himself he refilled his glass.

"Have you made the best of your short acquaintance?" he queried. "If not—I shall be happy to forward your projeĉt. But I assure you 'tis a hopeless case."

His sneering voice recalled me. "Indeed!" I replied: "I was unaware any projeĉt of mine had been committed to your care."

"Oh!" said he carelessly, "one can clearly see you love her; and I am willing to assist in the best way possible. Few know her so intimately:" and he traced some letters upon the polished oaken surface with a wine-besmeared finger.

His confident manner nettled me. "It is a great favour you would confer" I answered. "Yet in truth—it is now of little avail. Besides, your foot in this affair could not turn the scale."

He looked up quickly.

"Ho! ho! now I understand matters," he
cried; and, rising from the chair, my cousin
paced up and down the room. "'Tis delicious! she has given you, also, the short
shrift. Gad!" and, cackling with delight, he
perched himself upon the great lounge by the
hearth.

My face reddened, but I said nothing;
yet his words cut me, and I moved out from
the flickering firelight into the shadow.

"Ay," quoth he, "I was sure that would
happen. Play woman against woman,—and
the truth wells to the surface. But! what—
what am I to do with Doris?" "Why!"
said I, "what has she to do with this?"

He stared at me for a second, then burst
into a peal of laughter that rattled his ribs
against his stays.

"Lord!" he gasped, "what a dunce!
Doris? Why—everything!" and he fell a-
laughing again at some monstrous joke, but
losing his balance tumbled heels up into the
lounge.

'Twas humoursome to watch his thin
calves beat the air against the firelight, yet,
afraid he would hurt himself, I extricated him.

He smoothed his clothes, and sat down.
"Ah!" quoth he; "you fairly overcame me. Gad! I have it;" and he slapped his thigh. "Take Doris off my hands. Pray, do!" and he leaned forward with a simpering look upon his handsome face.

In a twinkle I had his purpose.
"Nay!" replied I gravely; "a man of the world, such as you, can surely handle two women at once."

He crowed. "Two!" cried he, snapping his fingers: "a round half dozen of 'em. "But I had thought now that Favilla has refused you, Doris would fill up the vacant heart. She's a pretty thing—brown as a berry—hair, head, and hands;" and he gazed pensively into the fire.—The withered up old fool!

But I heeded him not.
At last her name had rung upon my ears. "Favilla—Favilla"—and I repeated it softly to myself.

This world needs be a hostile place, when a beauteous woman cannot go forth, but there fall instantly differences between men; and for the most part betwixt old acquaintances.

Never had I held him in very great esteem, but now I hated the sight of him;
viewing his person with the same sort of eye
as we were in Tothill Fields to fight a duel.
I looked him all over, eyed him as he daintily
took a pinch of rappee and arranged his
ruffles, glanced at his profile as he turned to
me; and thought he looked a fool. But
women love to dangle a handsome idiot at
their petticoat strings.—Pshaw! a pretty
puppet for her to play with. Yet I liked
not even the idea of mere fooling, and would
he were at the devil.

He blew the snuff from off his laces, and
grinned to himself.

" I cannot understand why women love
me " he said complacently. " No! " quoth
I sharply; "nor I."

He moved uneasily in the chair at this,
then, reaching forward, lifted his wine-glass.
Meditatively he contemplated the ruby colour
of the port, as the firelight danced through
the facets and flashed sparks into the luscious
liquid. His lips fell apart, his brow wrinkled,
in truth, his age sat heavily upon him.

" Ay," he muttered, " one must pander

to them, flatter them to the top of their
bent; and they will aye be eloquent and
trustful."

"Are all women to be taken with that
bait?" inquired I sarcastically.

"Eh! what's that?" he cried: and I
repeated my query.

"No!" replied he with a faint cackle of
derisive laughter.—"There are exceptions.
But ply your trade according to the market,
and approach a woman upon her own level.
If she's wise: flatter her intellect.   If she's
an ass—well, flatter her, she is wise.—But
there are exceptions."

He sighed.   I smiled.

"Ah!"   I cried.   "You are in love in
earnest."

"Not I—not I," protested he most strenu-
ously.   "Indeed, I meant but an idle game;
and now she has swallowed hook and all.
What can I do with her?—Favilla! 'tis a
sweet name."   He paused, then jumped up.
"Gad!   I know—I'll marry her.—A fine
creature! Prithee cousin! wilt dance at the
wedding?" and smirking at me he left the
room.

His last idea must have tickled him, for, some short time after, when smoking in the bookroom, I heard his step crunch the gravel, and peeping out I saw him pass the corner gable, smiling prodigiously to himself.

Notwithstanding increasing dislike, I had to confess to his modish attire and goodly carriage. Indeed, with all his faults and years, he was yet as gallant a spark as could be found in Ranelagh Gardens on a fête night; and he knew it. One could not but notice the brave way he carried himself as he walked : I could have done that no more than fly. When passing out from the south lodge gates he chucked the porter's pretty daughter 'neath the chin, and kissed her too : I durst not have done that to save my skin.

" Ay," I groaned, "the country does make a bumpkin of one; " and I sat and railed at my lack of spirit.

At some distance behind the house was ranged a shady walk of aged beeches; and thither I went.

Cawing crowds of rooks slanted across the sunset sky, as they made for home; on the pasture land some lowing calves made the

quietness ring far and wide with their persistent cries; and in the distance the spiral
smoke ascending from the neighbouring ham-
lets proclaimed the stillness of the evening
air, that was only broken by the footsteps of
the wearied workers returning to their cots.

This avenue was a quiet and privy place;
and I gave full sway to my thoughts.

I was in love, beyond doubt. Favilla
—and my lips lingered upon the favoured
name—had captured my heart, carrying all
before her triumphant sway.

His offer of acquaintance opened up a
new train of ideas: prevailing love battled
against my pride.

As is easily imagined, I had no small
desire to meet her, and, if possible upon a
formed intimacy, accomplish my intention.
But to owe aught to him with his babbling
tongue and inordinate conceit! Nay, I
would give him no debt to charge me with,
but trust Dame Fortune to favour my
cause. Yet she lived in seclusion, so, only
through him did any approach appear to
me.

Before returning to the house I paused for

a while to gaze upon the landscape, as the gloaming gathered.

The sweet, earthy smell of newly turned sods from the adjoining ploughed fields, the noise of milking as with steady swish the milkers filled their coggies, the distant cry of a shepherd to his dog as it drove in the sheep, all were beloved of me: for I was only a country lout, unfamiliar with the delights of routs, masquerades, gadabouts, and the etceteras of St. James.

I was moving off, when, hearing voices, I tarried to discern the speakers.

" I assure you," I heard him say, " 'tis the shorter way—down by the beeches here, and along the field path—" " But the stile and barred gates "—a soft voice interrupted him—" I could never think to face them."

" Oh! " he rejoined, " one can surely help you."

" You will not be troublesome ? " was queried—" I know you of old."

I could fancy him snigger at this.

" Well! I must have payment," cried he : and they passed on.

Now is not love a subtle diviner. My

eyes had not seen, yet at once I wist that it was Favilla who had preceded with him. Instantly I apprehended his intent, and, giving way to bitter thoughts, manlike attributed all sorts of wiles to her.

" Who had imagined she possessed such coquetry ? " I cried desparingly. " Ay, women are all alike : they do but make man the tilting ground of folly. But Favilla—" ? and I was staggered at heart.

Then a suggestion occurred : maybe after all my hasty judgment was ill passed. So, curious from love and hatred, I sped down a covert lane to the field path.

In the dim light I could see they had halted before the first stile, and through the silent air their voices fell distinctly upon my hearing.

" I do not even know him " she said. " Why do you torment me ? "

" He has no acquaintance with you, then ? " he asked anxiously. " No ! " she replied sharply—" must I tell you that again ? Why do you question me so ? "

" He is in love with you " he cried fiercely. " You know that—no person need tell you the fool's case."

"He—he is in love with me?" she re-peated. "Am I to be held guilty for that?" and it seemed to me her voice rang softer.

"Favilla?" my cousin entreated: "Do you—" She interrupted him. "Pardon me?—Mistress Favilla. I had not known our acquaintance entitled any privileges." He heeded her not, but blathered on: "It is not of my cousin, but of myself, I wish to talk."

"Indeed," she remarked ironically, "do you ever talk of other folk?" "Ay," the blockhead answered, "sometimes about you."

"Such precious compliment" cried she, as she dropped a courtesy. "My Lord the beau hath bereft me of my wits:" and she burst into a peal of silvery laughter.

I had some notion that he would find himself in a sorry plight, for, so enwrapped was he in his conceit and pride that he per-ceived not the girl's fooling of him.

Suddenly mounting the stile she gained the other side. "Now we part," she said with a mocked sigh, and held out her hand to him.

"But you have some minutes' walk yet" he objected.

" Ah! I see, I must take care of you " she cried tenderly : " you have a delicate constitution to be abroad this damp evening."

The sarcasm was lost upon him.

" It is indeed good of you to think upon me " he exclaimed ; " but I did not reckon upon this speedy parting."

" 'Tis sad—but too true " she rejoined sententiously; and again proffered her hand.

" Listen to me " he mouthed. " You promised an answer to-night: and give 's it. My agony is unbearable."

She laughed provokingly.

" I know what you mean " she cried; " but the tongue must needs outrun your discretion."

Then she endeavoured to regain her hand.

" Nay, be not foolish " she exclaimed, as holding it to his lips he covered it with kisses. " Favilla," he murmured, " listen to my prayer." So in a rant of words he protested his passion.

She gave no sign of hearance. For a few seconds there was silence.

" Have you finished ? " she inquired in a calm voice. " The next time—prithee wait for encouragement:" and, snatching her hand away, she started back.

He attempted to regain hold, but the sudden, sharp flip-flip of her gloves against his cheek broke his ardour. Even at my distance could be heard the muttered curse from the beau, as he passed over the stile in hot pursuit.

Bursting with anger, I broke from the spot, and pressing in gained the apex of the angle where the paths converged.

He collided against me : my left shoulder sent him spinning into the dog roses upon the hedge. No need was there for apology.

He turned upon me. "How now, you d—d country numskull, must I always find you eavesdropping?" cried he; for he possessed a shrewd approximation of the truth.

In a moment of rashness he raised his cane —in a second it lay on the far side of the path.

"One needs have much leisure to stand by and listen to your idle chatter" I retorted warmly. "For whom did your arms gape across the stile? For Doris! Eh?" and I progged him with my stick.

He closed upon me.

"Come now!" quoth I : "be steady; and no mischief. Jove! the maid has scurried away." For my eyes could no longer discern the white robed figure flitting through the gloom.

"Tuts! tuts!" said I, "this is a sad case. Would Chloe suffer no favour from a city gent! Welladay, poor Cynthio!—What is the world coming to?"

"If you cannot hold your tonger—at least have sense" he muttered sullenly. "Your sudden presence took me aback" he added in an afterbreath.

"Ay!" replied I dryly; "one can see that."

And we returned homewards.

III.

THROUGH the haloed window panes of the upper gallery the young moon threw zigzag patterns upon the floor. I took a pensive pleasure in planting my footsteps aye in the same corners of the lighted patches; somewhat under the idea that so doing insured luck for my heart's desire.

Backwards and forwards I paraded the apartment's length. I cared not for the darkness, that, filling the long, empty spaces between the lights, looked so solid as to demand dispersion when I ploughed through it: the stir of thought within my brain made as though the place were full of sunshine; for I thought upon Favilla and her beauty.

Her tones dwelt in my memory.

"He—he is in love with me. Am I to be held guilty for that?" And the softening of her voice had exalted my hopes.

As I turned upon my heel, the north door opened, and some one entered.

I inquired, and was informed my cousin desired to see me. He had retired to bed, for, what between laziness and a desire to retain his complexion—he was as vain of his face, as any madam can be—he always ached for the luxury of the pillows.

As I entered, he looked up from sipping his cup of chocolate. Egad, he was a quizzical sight with a nightcap drawn about his wedge-shaped head, and an embroidered dress-ing-gown all as fine as the Turkish Bashaw's.

" You were asking for me " I said, as I threw myself into his padded seat. " Whew! this fire is scorching : " and I thrust myself from it.

He stared at me from tip to toe. " Yes! " he replied ; " 'tis about that girl. Who is to have her ? We had better settle the matter at once off the hand."

" Girl," quoth I, " which one—Doris ? "

" No," he answered, moving impatiently among his bedclothes ; " I mean not her, but Favilla."

" Well," replied I, laying the tips of my fin-gers together, and looking over them at him— "well, 'tis a question of preference, I'd suppose."

" She has money " he snapped out ; " and influence." " Oho! " I cried, " here 's the gist of the matter. And your bags require refilling, eh ? "

He glanced at me as if to slay me.

" I admit " said he, " money is a material consideration. Yet by Gad she is a fine woman —a fine woman. See here, Cousin Harry! After all, it is a risky business. Some folks say she's penniless, and the land passes to the uncle. 'Tis a risky affair" he repeated, meditatively rubbing his hands together.

"Nay! I'll not venture upon it" he continued: "I must have security for my person;" and wagging his head at the candles he lapsed into silence.

I glanced at his modish habiliments, then at the man himself. His sordid selfishness stung me; but he was a sodden piece of humanity, and what else could one expect? Yet, that one of my kin should act thus heated my blood.

"Suppose she were penniless" I cried, "what then?" and jumping up I went towards him.

He turned his shallow face upon me. "Lord!" quoth he. "I'd let her sink to what she would—a bagnio mistress:" and he chuckled as best he could without his teeth.

"Damn you!" cried I. "I'd marry her without a penny—in the shift she wears—if she has nothing else:" and I advanced upon him.

He withdrew beneath his bed-clothes; his face wore a new startled look upon it.

"Good God!" he muttered. "Take her then, take her—for you indeed love her."

And he turned his face to the wall.

IV.

FAVILLA could not rest. Upon the broad sill of the corner lattice stood a great Chelsea bowl filled with wallflower and jessamine. The rich perfumes spread out upon a current of air from the half-opened window; reaching her sensibilities they stirred up remembrance within her. She could not slumber. She tossed hither and thither upon her bed fain for sleep, yet it invaded not her eyes.

Among the green growths and creeping plants clinging to the outside stone was trained a great trail of eglantine, and, as the wind carried them, the odorous sprays flipped murmurous against the lattice panes.

Slowly the beat of her white forehead took earnest of the murmur, and resolved into the rhythm: "He loves—he loves you." She started. The words filled her ears:

" He is in love with you. No one need tell
his case." She smiled a little, then her face
grew sweetly grave. Had she not first noted
him, as she leant out from the hall window
and gathered the starry jessamine to mix with
hawthorn for the first of May?

And this recollection, quickened into existence by luscious fragrance, slowly blended
into the first notes of love's alarum.

He had not gone unnoticed. Ofttimes
had she observed him from behind the clinging veil at Dian's fountain, and, reckoning up
all things, he had found favour in her eyes:
that favour which is the progenitor of love.

Her face grew hot with maiden solicitude
at thought of that coxcomb's folly at the
stile: for her quick eyes had recognized her
lover on his sudden appearance, as womanlike
she looked behind.

Dimly realizing her burning cheeks were
indeed the signals of ripening affection she
strove to recall herself. This is absurd,
ridiculous, she thought, he is a stranger to
me: and she endeavoured to control her
heart's egregious conduct. Resolutely thrusting all thought of him from her, she recounted

the many suitors to her hand. Many gay sparks had knelt and vowed allegiance to her standard; yet easily had she blotted them from her memory's tablets. By reason of their number she deemed herself wondrous wise in men, and so fortified against sudden assault. In truth she was a veritable " Tomboy "—a sore romp trading in fickle hearts.

But now an indefinable feeling possessed her; and hidden love welled up, as not far off a restless dreamer murmured " Favilla " in his troubled sleep.

The recurrent heart carried her back to him, so, speedily forgetting past resolution, she indulged in unwary speculation.

" I may see him to-morrow," she murmured softly. " Dear, dear to-morrow!" And realizing the import of her surmise, blushing, she held her peace. Yet a tender fear of frustrated hope increased upon her; welding Love's shafts tightly together.

Behind the eastern ridge of Maisondieu dawn broadened upon the darksome sky. Narrow bands of gold gleamed in the slits between the sable clouds; as they brightened, the sullen vapours lightened and fell apart,

fleecy trails of crimson and purple floated
across the glowing gulf, and the clouds resolved into slate-coloured hue. Slowly the
sun peered over the bordering hills, and reft
in twain the veil of darkness on the valley's
bosom.

From a beechen hedge in the orchard a
blackbird flung his joyous, rich melody into
the ear of silent morn. Favilla found no
peace. She arose, and flinging covering on
leant out at the opened lattice.

Down in the laurel thickets rang an
amorous greeting to the lover's song: the
mellow strain fluting through the stillness
proclaimed Love's reign.

And Favilla hearkened with a tender smile
upon her parted lips. Then of a sudden she
hid her traitor face within the sweet shelter
of her hands.

May, 1894—*January*, 1896.

A LEMAN'S LOVE.

A LEMAN'S LOVE.

I. Issola again preferreth her Lover.

IN the garden close were no signs of life ;
not even a breath of wind to sway the
lilies to and fro. Now and again in the
outer air there echoed a stray voice and the
clink of an armourer's hammer, but no other
sounds disturbed the silence, and the afternoon drowsed on.

As lazy-footed Time crept along the
great shadow of the massive keep flung
across the sweltering flower-beds, a grateful
coolness tempered the heat, and birds emerging from leafy nooks made the air ring with
the music of their songs.

Issola awoke from her pleasing reverie.

D

Rising from beneath the shady tangle of briarwood, that clustered within the porch, she passed out overcome with sweet emotion. With lingering steps and languid eyes she proceeded over to the western rampart.

She slowly crossed the smooth green sward —ever and anon to stop shortly as if her senses were yet drugged with that love-sweetened meditation—to surge on again as present intent beat upon her. A bustling merle looked up from searching for a meal; it gave but a sidling peep then continued the engrossing task : from a gorbal high upon the tower the cooing gray dove saw her; swooping down it fluttered around, now and again to settle upon her shoulders. But enamouring thought still charmed her to oblivion ; and Issola strayed dreamingly across the flowery close.

At a turn of the steps leading to the upper terrace there grew a clump of fleur-de-lis; budgeoning like bursting flames in the darksome corner. Drawing nigh she plucked of them—unwittingly signaling her mis-fortune.

The terrace-top was gained. Crossing to

the narrow parapet, she overlooked the ramparts; then descending Issola lounged listlessly along them.

The teeth of time and war had sorely fastened upon the place. Here and there the walls were loose and crumbling, and ivy had encroached upon them; peace having reigned long in the land. Warfare had ceased with the new crown's accession. Its power was mighty at home and abroad; and the people grew fat with plenty. Indeed, all marvelled thereat. The common folk rejoiced and were content. Only the nobles murmured at the heavy hand of their successive rulers; none daring to do great acts of wantonness.—Any man could go his way without taking heed unto his neighbour.

Issola halted in her meandering: closing to the battlements she looked forth from a crenelle. A gentle breeze blew down from heather hills: soothing her heated brows it reinstalled cruel memory. The keen edge of ever poignant sorrow slashing the thin mantle of solacing fancy recalled her from happy dreamland. For a second the under-lip quivered; then, recollecting her tender message, she laid a burning face upon the cool gray stones of the narrow indent.

"Thy Love waiteth for thee with longing heart." As she crooned the words over the ardour of her passion broke in upon her—full of quickened emotion she held her breath.

Of a sudden, down upon the wind, came a quick rhythmical beat of galloping horses.

Issola started nervously at the unwonted sound : few knew of her in her upland solitude. And, tempted with rare expectation, she hurried down to the gateway.

As the stairway was reached noise of the great gates clashing clamorously together struck upon her hearing, and babble of apprehensive men-folk : so she tarried upon the upper steps much amazed at the occurrence. The left hand straying upon her encircling zone remorselessly crushed the yellow bloom; the expectant attitude revealed her heart's surmise : and Issola lingered by the first turn, pausing, yet poised for ready downward flight. Through a neighbouring machicolation the sun thrust in a glowing shaft : falling upon the arrested feet the ruddy dart burnished the sparkling buckles into fiery-eyed gold.

In her suspense Issola stared blindly at the
vivid flecks as they stood out against the dark
sandstone steps; yet she was intent on outside
matters, and, hearing Jellon's footsteps on the
stair, hastened down hoping against hope.

A grim smile gathered on the puckered
face of her aged retainer, as, stopping at a
loophole, he surveyed the approaching horsemen—his fingers instinctively hugging around
the hot sword hilt.   Hearing his lady's inquiry he relinquished his post to motion to
her to occupy it.

The sunlight poured into the narrow opening as if to overpower all vision ; a keen west
wind drove in with impetuous force : but
shielding her eyes with the palms of her
hands Issola peered eagerly down into the
wooded gorge, where ran the approach.
Nothing was to be seen.   Yet not far off the
track wound up to daylight; and now a gay
pennon fluttered in the breeze, a glint of ar-
mour flashed brightly ; then a small band of
horsemen defiled into easy sight.   With catching breath she endeavoured to discern the
emblem wrought upon the wavy streamer,
or devine the person of the leader.   But

glare of the sun blinded her sight, so she bade Jellon consider them.

He made out quickly the device of a boar carrying a torch between its tusks: perceiving this, he informed her. Torn with bitter disappointment and baffled expectancy, for a moment, she swung in the balance of tears ; then shame controlling her spirit immediate conjecture set in. In a trice the knight's purpose was apparent. The thought of his persistent endeavour brought the red blood to her pale cheeks, and repugnancy floating upon the high tide of anger swelled into sudden, vehement hatred. For Sir Guy, an assertive man and arrogant, would take no denial of his license, yet with frequent in-sinuation pressed his suit ; as she was but a woman, and defenceless.

Her heady temper broke forth. Stamping her foot, so the latchet flew asunder, she called Jellon to deliver her. " Tell him again " she cried shrilly, " I will have naught to do with a gallows-faced knight. Ay, he sounds before the gates now ! Has he not hawked his lanky limbs enough about me ? I had as lief marry a bastard ! " She ceased to listen to the trumpet's blare. "Ay, tell him the boar is best fitted for rutting in the mire: and need he know that? Away to him!" was panted out; and dizzy with rage Issola rocked slightly then reeled against the wall. Jellon sprang forward to uphold her: but recovering she in faint voice ordered him to deliver her message; so reluctantly he went from her.

Before the gates Sir Guy himself harangued, demanding admittance. The warder's stolid face betrayed no evidence of hearance—he but stared mulishly at the gaily caparisoned steed and its rider. The knight, overweening in self-conceit, grew enraged at the loon's high-stomached attitude. Drawing near to the archway, so near, that the tip of a lance could prick him, he essayed an attempt. Ere the keen point slid in between the iron bars the Jacksauce was gone, and he lunged into empty space; wellnigh overbalancing himself in this sally of impetuous foolery.

In a twinkle a scoresome of men lined the banquette above, and drawing held him at their mercy: for the knight was in light array and a craven heart to boot,—his men being distant two bowshot. Blind with rage at his ignominious position he was spurring towards his fellows, when Jellon thrusting a sour face over the battlements bade him stay; and fleering at the discomfited knight in taunting manner he discharged his message.

Sir Guy was all at a loss to reply. Indeed, the burden of it was too weighty for his immediate comprehension. As the import penetrated his numskull, he grew dumb with oblivious fury. Vainly he stuttered in reply —his chin but see-sawed the air. For the moment a notion of revenge bred fastly upon him, but he checked the insidious suggestion : scantiness of his following, moreso an all-reaching hand of kingly protection, defeated such project. So cursing, he turned horse and fled. Yet he brooded upon her outweighing repugnancy; and within his heart hatred of his rival ripened inchmeal into knavish intent.

  *   *   *   *   *

The noise of the retreating band beat in upon the hearing of Issola. She trembled slightly. As changed into stone she remained motionless against the wall listening with sharpened breath to the abating commotion. The receding sounds died away in the distance ; only the voices of her dispersing retainers were to be heard ; but, not until the approach of Jellon had she entire faith in the flight. Even then suppressed fear hung about her face—only to give way, as with much chuckling her trusty man-at-arms related the discomfiture of the violent knight.

Sir Guy found no favour in his eyes. It was with a significant nod that he declared him a cunning and base knight, a wary rogue;— was ever a shifty-eyed man not that? Did the Lady Issola not recolleƈt a raid into the north country? But she, cutting him short, bade him go, keep close watch ; and turning on her heel left him.

Jellon watched her, until rounding the corners of the lower tower she passed from view. From immemorial time his stock had served the name of De Vescis. Nay, was himself not the man, who with his lord had sustained the fame of England at Askelon: two men against the puissant infidel host. From sunrise to sunset the twain had held the tower against all comers : above their heads the free banner of England flapping in the languid breeze—below—that bloody stair choked with their slain.   But alas, when succour came, his lord was far gone by reason of many mortal wounds, and, babbling awhile of green England and a lone little maid therein he had died calling her name.

Jellon thought on this.   Pugh! once more that hot, fœtid stench, heavy with the stink of stale blood and ripped-up flesh, seemed to be puffed into his nostrils.   Full of the imaginary odour he gladly pushed his head through an aperture, and inhaled the sweet evening air.

Issola traversed the upper passages, hot with offence at Sir Guy's rampallion behaviour.   He held no place in her esteem. She loathed his gloomy face and lanky limbs. He had naught to recommend him save valour,—even that was tainted with suspicion. When first he had evinced his offensive attentions she treated him with gentle scorn, but encouraged by her loneliness and seeming neglect he had persisted in his uncivil conduct, notwithstanding much evidence of deep-rooted opposition.

With beating heart and passionate thoughts she considered his repeated insult. The coward! to fasten his detestable company upon a defenceless woman. Clenching soft hands she could have slain him, had he been by her, so beside herself was she with anger. Never at any time had she mentioned aught to Sir Raoul, for he, being a passionate man, was ever ready with hand on sword: then, the lust besotted knight might be spit like a mammocked woodcock before his burning dwelling. She had no fear of him. None durst assail or lay hands upon her. For the King rode roughshod over the land, and all the barons feared his stern authority.

Close by, at the end of the passage, was a covert chamber built within the wall. Issola turned in thither clean forespent: resting upon the broad embrasure of an unbarred bole she gazed down into the emblazoned west. By degrees her shadow sank into the wall whereon it was cast; the crimson afterglow on the far horizon thinned away; and labouring lines of rooks made loops of flight as they homed to the wooded uplands. No stir was in that darkening chamber. Only Jellon's gruff voice floated up from the ramparts as he went his rounds.

The damsels searching for their mistress encountered him, and fruitlessly inquired of her. None had seen aught of her since early afternoon; and with lurking apprehensions they questioned him. He could bestow no information, but, thinking for a little, he bade them stay until his return : hastening through the lower tower to no avail he turned to regain the open ;—passing by the covert chamber he discovered her. Exhausted and weary Issola had fallen asleep with her aching head resting on soft arms crossed upon the cold, stony sill. Jellon stepped forward to awaken her. Some tears yet glistened upon the fair eyelashes, but a tender smile possessed her face. " Raoul, dear Raoul," was murmured in a passing dream ; then, sighing heavily, the dreamer sobbed a little in her troubled slumber.

A tightening feeling gripped Jellon by the throat as he listened to that gentle whimper. He recollected, it was, when sitting by his dying lord's side waving a withered branch of palm to cool the heated forehead that last he had listened to such sound. The knight's wagging tongue had clattered in his closing moments of his little maid, as once one summer's day she had sat in a meadow prinking him with buttercups—he had whimpered lightly—then tossing himself up had cried mightily "Issola! Issola!" and died. A curious feeling came over the hardened man-at-arms as he thought on this: speeding off, he returned with soft covering, which he gently threw about his undisturbed lady; withdrawing, he sent a handmaid to await beside her.

A little time passed, a gate clanged, a few footsteps rang in the air; then silence. This attracted Jellon's attention, and he proceeded without. Suddenly the inner door of the outer hall was opened upon him, and a little page rushing in fell headlong against him. Florimel was staggered by the shock, but not a tittle was his ardour abated; pulling impetuously at his opponent's jerkin he besought him for information of his mistress.

Ere Jellon had time to reply, Sir Raoul stood before him. He likewise inquired. But the lad, eager to inform his ignorant lady,

hearkened to the first words, and fleeting off
before them burst in upon the startled handmaid. From a niche in the wall a low
burning wick sent out a fitful radiance—now
the shadows played upon the sleeper's face—
now upon her form. Perceiving she slum-
bered the boy halted, irresolute of his behaviour. Her lover solved all doubts.

He had stopped at the threshold : the
light only showing a glistening gown white
against the dark gray wall. One glimpse was
enough ; and he sprang forward. As he
bowed down to touch her lips Issola twitched
somewhat, and awakening, peered vacantly
into his face. She rubbed her heavy eyelids ;
a puzzled look flashed across her countenance.

Sir Raoul bent back a little, confounded
at her strange manner. "Say, I have not
dreamt it then ? " she cried ; and leaping up
with a whinny of delight nestled within his
outstretched arms. So Jellon slunk off
quietly with her damsel at his heels.

II. Her Lover Meeteth a Shameful Death.

SIR RAOUL was chained tightly to Love's chariotwheels. He cared not for the wind nor rain, that lashed about the turrets of the sullen donjon : leaning against the upper parapet he stared eastward into the black, blustering night. He had no thoughts, but for Love's consideration. A blinking moon threw darts of light across the marshy plain to reveal the mist-filled hollows of the uplands, but scurring cloud flew in tangles across the beaming disc, and forbade his impatient gaze.

Down in the keep his lady-mother sat pricking upon her broidery-frame ; yet the scallop shell grew slowly on the pilgrim's bonnet, and the silken weft ravelled thickly in the red Venetian cloth. Ever and anon she glanced at the fair face of Lady Elaine, who sat at her feet reading aloud the story of Paladin Roland and his knights fighting

against the Saracens.   And, as the history
related of valorous fighting, the high-spirited
maid—living in the strife—retold the tale
with heightened colour and ennobled voice,
her blue eyes aglow with excitement.   The
hoarse winds grew high ; great gouts of rain
poured against the shuttered boles ; storm-
fiends screeched in the darkness without : but
peace within that chamber was exceeding great.

In the upper hall the fir faggots blazed
and crackled with long-tongued flames, send-
ing a furnace blast up the capacious chimney ;
massive carvings of stone threw grotesque
shapes upon the arras as the torches flickered
in the draughts ; and strange shadows wavered
in unlit corners as the fires waxed and waned.

The knight crossed the reeds with feverish
haste.   Standing beneath a guttering flam-
beau   he   re-read   her   loving   message :
"Issola longeth for thee."   Like one overcome by ripened wine he swayed with
lavish passion, then bending down he pressed
his lips against such foolish, sweet words.
Delicate perfume of her dear hands yet
lingered about the tiny scrip.—With instant
insinuation his memory was stirred.

While once he reclined close listening to
the stir of her silken bodice, Issola had reached
forth to a golden pouncet-box, and, laughing
in her glee, had shook the smiling Cupid's
face, sprinkling sweet perfume upon his locks.
—Without, gay peacocks strutted in the sun,
the flowers leaned amorously to the breeze, and
joyous life forgot the creeping feet of Death.

The storm chapped about. Faint gusts of
wind penetrating within thrust forward the
hangings, whereon was enwoven the story of
Troilus and Cressida arising from their first
love sleep, whilst Pandar entered upon them.
This spectacle jarred against Sir Raoul's rapt
affection. He advanced towards the hearth :
glowering into the fantastic, curling flames
he pondered with swithering desire fluxing
in his hot veins. Her message recurred. As
a coiling snake amorous recollection encased
about his heart, and stifled all compunction.

He thirsted for her. " O God! God!" he
murmured. " How sick I am! If only she
were by me now.—Heaven holds naught so
sweet as my heart's delight." Had he not
wooed in the year's month of lilies—wooed
Issola in the blossoming orchard close? With

E

the first shy kiss she had impressed her sovereignty upon him; sealing Fate's records.
Only to be nigh her for one—one hour!
None would know. And did she not wait for
him?—he must go. So passionate madness
impelled him through the sour night to her.

In the narrow cleft of Caldersheugh a
bundle of wet spears stacked against the rock
gleamed in the fitful moonlight; on an eddy
of the wind came sounds of hoarse voices
and clang of armed men.

Sir Guy walked apart from his followers,
and cursed the lengthy wait. Baulked desire
spiced the baseness of his purpose, making
him weary until his end was accomplished.
"Sir Cravenheart!" he muttered. "The rain
daunts him.—A petty lover! 'Twould cool
his heated blood." And he laughed coarsely.

The wind sank; the rain ceased: a deep
silence fell upon the land: and the hunch of
Caldersheugh loomed big in the uncertain
light.

From out the thickness of overhanging
cloud sprang the murmuring of a moan: that
moan of lamentation from souls lost in the
desolate land whence is no return. And a

great fear overspread all that heard. The
sounds died away. Only the quavering calls
of startled moorbirds recorded witness of the
strange visitation.

Sir Guy halted on his heel, shuddering
with unacquainted terror; crossing himself
he hurried to his rogues, who, springing
up, had clustered together, the dice lying unheeded at their feet. But the dull ears of
Sir Raoul hearkened not—he rode on tram-
melled with conceits.

As at Love's feast he lay beside his beloved,
while she dropt the luscious fruit between his
empurpled lips. Fine samite winding loosely
about unguardedly revealed her tender body
to his audacious eye; the jewelled girdle
tightening against her low, sweet bosom
thrust forward the blush roses slipped down
betwixt her budding breasts. She pressed
fragrant hands upon his beating temples, and
drew up the passionate face nearer and nearer
to her own, until his hot lips closed against
the cool white throat : his arms twined about
her slender shoulders, and he munched the
honey of her mouth.

His jennet made slow progress in the

quaggy track ; its feet clatching heavily in the muddy ruts. It stumbled on through pools of standing water : the splashing plods awoke the curlews' weeping wail, and their eerie cries sounded about him, as they wheeled and doubled in the darkness above.

Of a sudden Sir Raoul was plucked from his saddle : a hot, clamouring burst of men surrounded him. They tore him to the ground. Bearing upon the knight they endeavoured to bind him ; but wrestling mightily in a moment he freed himself.

The knight fought bravely. 'Twas parry and thrust—speedily the bloody steel cleared a way. A chance blow shattered it. Striking at his foes with bared hands he clove a passage. A fierce fury broke out in him. Clutching two bodies—the twain nearest him—he smote their heads together, bursting them like bastard nuts. Their fellows afeard at this for a second withdrew, the knight rushing upon them as one possessed of devils. His foot tripped. In a trice they were on him : all falling upon Sir Raoul they had smothered him as he sprawled on the heath.

Then outside the hubbub a cruel voice

cried sharply : " Bind him, bind him, rogues ;
and bring him thither!" But no man
struggled—'twas a maddened fiend. None
durst so much as leave off him to pick up
the entangled ropes. Sir Guy jeered at his
lozels ; treading forward softly he directed
them. "How now, loons !" he snarled.
" Have the wits left ye ? Pin him by
nether limbs to the ground." His men thrust
at the knight with their lances, and pegged
his writhing body to the turf. At last they
bound him amid jibes and much cursing.

Now Sir Guy strode forward, and, shoul-
dering his loathly face so near that his hot
breath stunk in the nostrils of his victim, he
taunted him, mocking him of his dear love.

Sir Raoul recognizing the fell purpose in
hand prayed with sickly soul for his beloved ;
but never spake he a word.

They dragged him to a lone fir tree, pricking him with their cruel spears so that the
red blood guttered down his bespattered side ;
hooting him they bade God speed his unshrived soul.

As he lay beneath the withered branches,
panting and exhausted, impotently striving

to escape his bonds, lo, a vision filled his eyes of a sweet bowed down face with yellow hair, even as he had first beheld his leman in the summer of her youth: and his heart cried unto that hidden face.

At the midnight hour they cast a halter about his neck, and striking from off his feet the golden spurs they hung him, until the cool hands of Death calmed his jerking body.

III. Hatred Slayeth Itself.

Daylight faded away; and the twilight deepened into dusk. In the thickets upon the hill night birds fluttered uneasily about at sounds of an approaching traveller.

Sir Guy urged his sorrel upward, but the tired steed scrambled and sprawled upon the stony track, and progress was tardy. Already the knight had repented of his foolish freak. Yet, as he twisted in and out among the ragged pines that lined the hilltop, he cast furtive glances to the right and left of him.— Maybe the restless dead yet roamed upon the earth, as in days of yore; who knew?

At length the hill scaled he descended to the plain. Thick mist rising from the marshes between the mountain ranges veiled the entire neighbourhood ; but aware that his steed required no guidance, slackening the reins, Sir Guy engaged in recriminating thought.

Was there ever such timorous fool ? to hatch the notion of a revengeful spirit was the action of a madman's brain ! Yet, as he cast the matter over in his mind, again the weird suggestion crept upon him ; so muttering an oath he spurred forward.

*   *   *   *

Some time ago this strange idea had been begot, and, dwelling within his head had softly encaved there. One day, when musing with himself, the lurking affection had sprung into existence ; catching upon the attention it had employed his faculty : but never until the present had it much menaced him.

During the past afternoon, while flying his merlin at some small birds of the air, this insidious proposition had ripened into full conception, had surged upon his intellect and being ; soaking into the tissues of superstitious credulity it had wholly possessed him.

The young spring sun flickered its fiery flashes upon the yellow furze as a breeze drove forward the fleecy clouds; the bird of prey hovered above its quarry; and as a leveret sped by his hounds strained fiercely upon their leashes. But Sir Guy had heeded not—all immersed in sudden horrid conjecture he stared blankly before him. Not until the merlin's prey fell headlong at his feet had he regained control. He shrugged his shoulders. " Bah ! " quoth he, " 'tis all that packald of lies Outram recounted last night —old wives' tales ! " and picking up the hooded quail he had turned him homewards.

But he could not rest within the keep or outer works : a subtle, insinuating fear slowly enwrapped about him, precluding all peace.

He had entered the lower hall, and drawing nigh to a settle within the fireplace sat doggedly down. A few green logs lay smouldering upon the open hearth ; now they burst into flame, now they hissed and bubbled as the heat drove out the sap. The perturbed knight carelessly eyed them, sometimes turning over the charred bark upon the embers to watch it catch fire and flare up.

He smiled. Had he not that pair of golden spurs hanging upon the wall above his pallet? Certes, he had never obtained that lot save by their wearer's death! Again he smiled; but his face wore a sorry twist. —Was ever mortal plagued with such capricious imaginations?

Mere cogitation had strengthened his prevailing fantasy. Until, surely ever surely, there arose the fixed conviction :—Sir Raoul was yet alive.—Had he ever slain him?

In a burst of unmanly terror the knight had sprung from the seat, and hurriedly gained his sleeping chamber. The fool!—There, before his eyes, hung the dead man's rowels beaming in a narrow ray of sunlight: he had but to take four steps, and his fingers touched them.

So bereft was he of his wits that he had covered his vision. Maybe when next he looked, they might not be there—this might be mere illusion. For a few moments he had stood wavering in nervous uncertainty, then peered betwixt his disclosed fingers: the

lustrous spectacle still greeted his sight.
Leaping forward with a shrill cry of delight
he had fingered them; pressing his thumbs
against the sharp pricks; and dulling their
bright surfaces with his sweaty palms.

Unbidden memories returned upon him :
he was again by Caldersheugh on that sour
October night. Once more he stood beside
that murderous scene. And as in the silence
of the midnight, when watching with savage
joy the squirming body of his rival he had
heard the harsh crake of winging mallards,
again, these grating sounds struck upon his
hearing.

Sir Guy started : he had sworn Sir Raoul
was by him now. And this sensation pouring
in upon him, he had slunk hastily from the
chamber.

His suspense increased with the growth
of time; until, intermingling with dire suspicion, it had driven him on a fruitless
errand.

As he crossed the hills, spring sunshine
and fresh breezes had allayed his excited
emotions : but to physic all disease indubit-
able evidence of his eyes was requisite; and

he held upon his way. His courage reviving, he had jeered at his cowardly self; he swore, 'twas lack of fresh air and exercise—house-room was but for womenfolk. Thus railing at himself and the times he had discharged his cowardly bile.

At length skirting round the foot of Caldersheugh Sir Guy had struck off in a westerly direction; discerning in the distance a lone fir tree he turned towards it. Beneath the sapless branches lay a decaying corpse defiling all sweetness of the evening air. The knight had reined in his steed, and looked at this unwholesome spectacle.

A monstrous black mammet was perched on the mortifying body; feasting upon the stinking carrion. Never before had Sir Guy seen the like; and he glanced uneasily at it. The bird peered at him, then flapping its heavy wings endeavoured to fly; but heavy, overcome with rancid flesh, it could only hop upon the ground. Hirpling a little way off it had croaked evilly at the intruder.

It had edged towards him with sidling limp; ever and anon dabbing its beak against

the clods to relieve it of clinging shreds of
flesh : but aye it had come the nearer. Blinking furiously with its unblinded eye it had
fascinated the luckless mortal.

Some time in the far bygone—in the depth
of ante-natal years—had he not witnessed this
scene. That corpse. That bird. Nay, there
upon the murdered's face lay the strange fleece
of golden hair overhiding all semblance of
countenance.

The knight had glanced from the body to
the bird ; until, enthralled by the foul mes-
senger of Tisiphone, he gazed fixedly at its
baleful eye gleaming with the hidden cunning
of many centuries.

The sun had sunk ; the sky grew overcast
with sullen clouds ; a low wind moaned as it
sifted through the branches of the blighted
tree.

The mammet had hopped nigh to its
transfixed victim. Still chaining the brain
with malignant subtilty it had fluttered on
his bosom ; then clambering up it settled
beneath his chin. Their eyes met.—Sin spake
of sin : Destiny of her decrees. Rendered
presumptuous the beastly fowl had raised

itself up, and pecked viciously at his strained countenance; but failing to reach had fallen screeching to the earth.

The sorrel, startled by the sudden noise, had reared from the fearsome object at its feet. The motion jogged Sir Guy. He had started—and having gazed wildly around him spurred in terror from the spot. He had pressed away so impetuously, that not until crossing Skaithmuir Law had his former erratic notion again overwrought him.

*　　*　　*　　*

As now he cantered and reviewed the matter, his ghostly apprehensions revived and weighed heavily upon him. Was not the thing possible? did not the tale of Sir Brian and Yvenec, his paramour, prove such fact? Thus, while he'd fain shatter the argument, he but adduced proof.

Time went by; and he neared the mouth of the valley where lay his stronghold. Happening to glance upwards he noticed a ruddy glare shoot into the dark sky. A exclamation burst from his lips. He stopped, and stared gapingly upon the night clouds;

then, in another instant clapped spurs to his
horse. He turned the corner of the crags.
A band of furious men surged within his
castle walls; the outworks were in flames;
and from all sides went up the din of battle.
The knight dashed forward, but a moment's
reflection cooled him; he could effect nought;
yet curiosity prevailing he abided a little.

The north side of the great court burned
brightly, and revealed the mass of fighting-
men as they surged to and fro in mortal
combat. Slowly the enemy crushed the castle-
men into a corner, and slew them at their
leisure. And Sir Guy, absorbed in the strife,
gradually made his way along the ridge,
till he stood within four bowshot of the
place.

Fresh foes swarmed in, and gave short
shrift to the garrison. In the south corner
of the quadrangle only one stood alive: his
halbert making bloody work as he parried and
chopped at the seething mass of enemies before him. At last one running in fetched
him a cruel blow beneath the oxter; and he
dropped like a stone.

The foemen turned their attention to the

keep. Finding it impregnable, they ceased assaulting; but firing brushwood and dampened litter before the doors they had stifled and burned alive the trembling inmates. The scared women and children crowded upon the leads, while the few aged men-at-arms essayed a vain attempt to quench the fires.

The flames gripped hold: flickering, beating, their long tongues against the stout oak they crept within. On the upper stair the hindmost occupants shoved fiercely against their fellows; yet packed tight upon the roof, none could give way—each wedged in the other.

The fire crawled up the winding stairway and caught upon the woollen hose and long brown tresses of a maddened woman. On all sides oozed up thick, acrid smoke choking the lungs; while darting sheets of flame beat upon the faces of those jammed against the parapets.

Suddenly a figure leapt out from an overhanging embrasure—to drop upon the spear points below. Heavy locks of hair blinded an archer's face as it fell with a dull thud against him: and some looking upon the woman's fair countenance repented of her death.

Craven heart though he was, Sir Guy had fain charged into that cowardly throng, yet discretion taking the upper hand he edged away. What was that hovering beneath the dense cloud of smoke that stretched as a pall overhead? now it swooped down even into the exulting flames—now it soared above the doomed stronghold. 'Twas the mammet. Through the uproar of the conflagration came its harsh, mocking notes; to thrum upon the ears of Sir Guy as his knell song.—The knight fled headlong into the pitch black night unwitting of any path.

✻   ✻   ✻   ✻

The hours sped on. Tired and exhausted the sorrel plodded onward unsteadily; its rider keeping wary watch around him. The waste-lands had been reached; there was no chance of surprise: but his quaking heart got no relief. Now he heard noises to the left of him, now to the right; and as often did the knight clap hands to his sword to find that beastkind alone disturbed him.

F

He durst not think upon the day's ploy:
it had fairly unnerved him. Even the catas-
trophe of the night scarce aroused him from
his apathy; yet as he travelled on, his brain
recounted the incident of that afternoon.
He pondered upon it. The affair was indeed
an odd occurrence. The more he thought
on't, the less he liked it: it savoured of evil;
and rankling, sorely disturbed his peace of
mind. Hasty speculation called up all man-
ners of omens, and sought to attribute certain
interpretations: nevertheless he could cast
upon nothing.

As he cautiously picked his way among
the boulders a signification pierced his wits.
It fastened in his brainpans; jogging a re-
luctant memory it verified itself.

Long years ago, when he was a curly-
headed lad with babbling tongue, had not the
wizard of Pendleton told his weird? And
now, every tittle of that telling was fulfilled.
—A mouldering corpse with golden hair—
a loathly bird of calamitous omen—a hearth
aflame from its own fire: thus had the
ancient prognosticated the falling hand of
Fate. And as one recalls a spent event by

means of trifling detail, so Sir Guy remembered, that as he cowered behind his father, the latter had snatched some ducats from his pouch and flung them in the seer's face— with no good result—for the mannikin but cursed him with greater vehemence than before.

All this thronged into the knight's head as he steered haphazard amongst the rocks, until emerging from the gorge he gained the lower tableland. Thick darkness filled the immense space and settled as a blanket upon the face of the earth ; here no creature moved, not even a breath of wind.

Some sense of coming danger stirred within Sir Guy, and he checked his horse ; but about him there was no sound or token—naught but stark darkness. He went on a little way, then stopped.

Alone, in the midst of black night that swallowed up all life, an intolerable suspense ripened within him.

The chance movements of his sorrel accentuated the stillness of the place. So intensely did they re-echo the desolateness of his situation, that he durst not listen to the sounds as they beat against the silence which inclosed about him.

The constraint of night weighing heavily upon him grappled his soul with an overmastering hand; even until it had mortified all reason. His imagination ran riot. The atmosphere did palpitate with something indefinable—with an unnamed horror. So in burst of pent dread, setting spurs to his steed, the knight rode off swiftly as if before pursuit. The wizard's forecast gathered in his head, and enfevered the distraught condition of his mind. He could not thrust it away : it burned heavily into his soul : it shook manhood from him. Again the air quivered with that throb of impalpable horror. Impelling against Sir Guy it quenched all hardihood in him : and weighted with mysterious fear the miserable knight crawled on through the swathing darkness.

Now behind him was to be heard the noise of a galloping horse. The sounds became more distinct—they were approaching ; he could hear the clatter of hoofs upon the pebbly track. A pleasing sense of human fellowship filled the knight, and he loitered.

As the horseman drew nigh Sir Guy's sorrel stirred uneasily ; the stranger advancing, it grew more restive ; now and again it plunged forward to be checked with tightened curb.

The knight was withdrawing a little to his left when an instant scare seized him from tip-to-toe : beast and man took sudden fright, and scurried in panic from the spot. Yet they shook not off the coming horseman— the quick thud of hoofs followed on. His sorrel wallowed in the marshy soil, but Sir Guy gave no respite; intent on flight he drove his rowels the deeper into the brute's bespattered flanks. But aye he heard the oncomer behind. . . .

Now could he scarce rely upon his ears ;— silence reigned about. He stopped. Nothing was to be heard save the hard panting of his steed. He collected himself. Was ever such an idiotic fool ! To run from one unbeknown was the action of an erratic.—Was he mad ? Even with that there came a rush of wind— the hoarse breathing of a hard-pressed horse —the thunder of his hoofs. Petrified with a monstrous terror the knight could not budge. The hot nostrils of a jennet scorched

his thighs; and the impetuous rider fled by.
In passing, that one uncovered the face.—
With a great shriek Sir Guy flung hands
upon his eyes. . . .

In the heavens the sable clouds had rolled
away; starlight now gleamed in the dewy
cups of heatherbells; and on the zodiac the
slanting signs betokened the expiry of stubborn night.

Sir Guy's steed browsed upon the scanty
foggage; moving hither and thither it ate its
fill. As it cropped the dewy grass some
daring rodents hopped nigh to nibble at a
juicy herb, or play at hide-and-seek in and
out about the horse's feet, for no one heeded
them. Sir Guy sat motionless in his saddle
—erect, staring straight before him, he seemed
to question the gloom of its evil deeds. Some
hours past he had not stirred, nor had he
spoken. The sorrel grew restive. It whin-
nied; twitched at the bridle rein: but there
was no response. It moved on; stopped;
pawed a little; then neighed loudly to the
twinkling stars. Sir Guy awoke. Like one
relieved from oppressive dreams he shuddered—drew a hand across his brows—and

looking vaguely around went slowly on his way.

He had gone a few miles, when in the distance again echoed the dull reverberations of a rider hurrying on his track.

A deathly sensation benumbed the knight: it was as though his being had slipped away, leaving behind naught but the husk of a refuse body. Passively he awaited the arrival ; as one inert ; as one devoid of self-action. His horse broke fruitlessly away. Speedily the fierce rider was with him : reining in, that one tarried by the knight's side—stride for stride—motion for motion. A prodigious terror paralysed Sir Guy; he durst not lift up his eyes nor thrust his tongue upon the audacious horseman : but rode as one bereft of all reason. Thought of that uncovered face haunted him, till he was monstrously maddened. The air was full of its multitudes: they flew alongside him : they lined the plain from end to end. He shut his eyelids : they danced within them. Until, verging upon lunacy, he broke open his lips ; and cursing and blaspheming the knight flew across the land.

Yet ever was he conscious of that strange

horseman by his side. And the twain swept through the fast dwindling darkness: the murdered and his victim. . . .

Down in the dales the cocks crew early morning to their cackling mates.—Like to a waning shadow the wraith fell apart, and was gone: and the knight galloped on alone.

His sorrel slackened its pace. Rounding the edge of Caldersheugh it proceeded leisurely in an easterly direction.

Upon a far-away ridge of hills the great rose of dawn blossomed, growing larger and larger, until the gray sky above was flecked with red and yellow cloudlets; the stars faded away; and larks sent up their songs of joy into the ear of wakeful morn.

On a neighbouring knoll, outlined against the ruddy east, stood a lone fir tree; from the upper branches of which a few shreds of rope dangled loosely in the freshening breeze.

Sir Guy drew nigh. Suddenly he raised his head. His imbecile eyes roving upon the ground alit upon the corpse of a slain knight; and he halted. Then the tongue babbered within his mouth. " His face! his face!" he cried shrilly; and swaying unsteadily in the saddle fell headlong to the earth.

The sun arose and ran its course: and darkness again gathered upon the lands to shroud a plunging steed tethered to the dead man's hand.

IV. Issola Redeemeth the Unshrived Soul.

Winter had come and gone; spring had passed: and night began to shorten the numbers of her hours.

Within the narrow precincts of the garden close Issola walked with her handmaids, and enjoyed the perfumed air. An eventide breeze wavering among the fragrant plants and shrubs mingled the varied scents into one generous pervading odour; the mating doves were at ease; and all Nature rested for the coming night.

As the chattering band gathered upon the grass, one of the damoselles passing by a bunch of love-at-ease snatched a bloomy spray, and, pulling apart the satin petals enacted playfully "He loves—he loves me not." The others collected about her; yet Issola went slowly onwards, her eyes bent upon the ground as engaged in weighty thought. She paid no heed to the laughing cluster of sprightly maidens as they stood about the luckless flower bespoiling it of every pinken blossom, but holding straight on attained the west terrace stairs. Passing up them she reached the outer ramparts.

The sun had sunk beneath thick lowering clouds, gilding long inner streaks into thin golden lips; the glow smote the sky, and it gloomed redly as daylight waned. A waft of wind moved the sable yewtips in the close with solemn motion, then ceased; and sombre stillness held the air as evening closed in.

Issola paused for a moment, then stepping to the banquette leant against the battlements. She took tent to naught, but gazing steadily down into the west seemed lost to all externals.

The damoselles hastening after her poured along the terrace, all laughing and merry-hearted: but Issola—her face bowed upon her hands. "His love hath been won away from me," she moaned, "for yet he cometh not, nor tidings of him." And recalling tender love-passages she wept piteously.

From a watch-tower in the upper rampier
the maidens saw her; hurrying down by the
north entry they sped to her, thinking to tell
her of their fortunes. Of a sudden, hearing
the sound of weeping, they stopped—all
hanging against the wind like so many pen-
dulous white blossoms; then softly they went
towards her, and with gentle words sought
to appease her grief. Issola lifted her tear-
sodden countenance, and speaking sweetly
bade them return to the keep, where she also
would in little time rejoin them. With hushed
voices they retired; but Guinivere lingered
behind, for she loved her mistress.

Again these tired eyes, weary of watching,
were strained forth to the lowlands, as if to
seek from them her beloved wherever he
was. But the glimmering landscape was
slowly hidden under murky gloom; in Duleswater wrack arose, and thickened over that
desolate valley; the blue deepened above;
and stars lit up their tiny tapers. Her yellow
locks grew dank with dew; and the kirtle
clung with weighty folds about her. Yet,
heedless of the time or place, her stricken
heart went from her in heavy sobs. " 'Tis

the third month," she wept, "and he hath
never come. His love is dead : " and she
nursed sorrow upon pangs of sweetened recollection.

He had wooed with the last year's lilies.
His amorous persuasion had dulled away into
the hum of drowsy bees seeking honey from
her flowers, as he took her within his arms
and pilfered passion from her ruddy lips; for
she could not deny him. Month had glided
into month, and they dallied long with love's
delight. Now winter had merged into spring,
and spring was breaking into summer, yet he
had not crossed the threshold of her bower,
nor, had any heard his footsteps in the halls.
Death—death often strode along these lonely
uplands : but she quenched the vauncing
thought. " He is not dead " she cried.
" For none durst stand against him." She
bethought herself of his lusty strength and
noted prowess in the field ; but wist not of
enemies lying in secret wait.

Now Guinivere crept forward, and with
delicate persuasion entreated her to with-
draw. Issola hearkened; and the twain turned
thence to the keep. Worn out with grief,

that bade fair to envenom as death's poison, she passed straightway to her bower.

A lamp borne between the wings of a silver cherubim flickered in the draughty chamber, and shed a heady perfume on the air. Through a barred rose window the rising moon threw warm gules upon the floor, and stained the rushes as if with new spilt blood.

Issola, sick at heart, had no patience for the tattling of her handmaids, and dismissed them in short terms; then crossing to a settle she flung herself down on the gray wolf's skin.

The emblem of a bleeding heart resolved itself within the moonlit circle upon the reeds; for a second it held there, and was gone. But her eyes beheld not. And a dense cloud arose out of the west and covered the face of the moon.

Her heavy head craved for rest ; and she unrobed. The light flamed up, and revealed on the corded hangings Tristram and Iseult of Tyntagel enthroned by Love in Heaven. They stared compassionately at the world-old grief; but the elves behind the scarlet wolf grinned with jealous glee.

" His love is mine " she murmured; " for

what of this body, his eager arms so oft enclipt": as the fine gauze of a last covering
betrayed her exquisite shape.

A mighty gust of overwhelming passion
broke out, enflaming her hungered heart:
and it raged with restless stour. Would she
not forswear all heavenly hopes to feed her
thirsty lips upon his sweet mouth and feel
his cool arms enclasp with strenuous embrace?
Even hell would she endure for his sake—
Nay, no pain or anguish were possible to be
sharper than the present—if only she could
reach him—.

In a frenzied burst of amorous desire she
cast herself upon her couch crying upon the
name of her beloved.

The night passed on ; and the twelfth hour
drew nigh. The starry eyes of an asp on the
glittering catch of her warm and fragrant
zone gleamed with baleful fire, and the elves
sprawled over the precious stones and dived
among the fastnesses of her snowy lawn. A
great gray owl flew up from the lowlands,
and perching upon the sill hooted three times
before her bower window. It paused for an
instant, then swooped down into the darkness

beneath. The sounds awoke Issola. She arose :
slipping like a snow-white fawn across the
rustling reeds she threw open a shot window,
and looked forth. The nightbird fluttered up
silently to the sill; seeing her it dipped off;
hooting hideously in its wavering flight it
swayed away, and was lost in the depths of
night. And the sands of the twelfth hour ran
slackly.

Suddenly the heart stirred tumultuously
within her. "Yea, he cometh!" she cried:
but there was no noise or signal of approach.
A light hand tirled three times on her door;
and she lagged forward to unlatch it. The
door swung open. Lo, it was he she exalted
before all men. Issola flung herself upon
him. "Love—My love!" she cried shrilly;
and entwined close about him murmuring
words of delirious joy. So bestraught was she,
that speech failed her—she could but lie upon
his dear bosom.

"Beloved, where have ye been of past
months?" at length she whispered, looking
up into his face. His white lips moved
in speech, but she sealed them to silence.
"Stay, stay," he cried, "the hour speeds;

and God's day is at hand. Hear my prayer, that I may go hence with peace for all time." "Our folly is our delight" she answered softly : and with love's cozenage she allured him to dalliance.

Sir Raoul touched not the wanton. "Sweet Leman," said he, "many nights have ye bewailed thy love; and now from walking to and fro upon the face of the earth have ye called me. What will ye? Alack, my love is now as Death's cold breath, and my kisses as the echo of his voice." But she interrupted him.—"Talk of love's joys ;—thy lips are aye sweet to me."

The moon shone from behind the cloud; one ray falling in struck upon the Crucified in the chamber chapel, and Christ stared upon them. The light veiled its face: and the sands of the hour-glass slowly ceased to run.

The eyes of her lover glowed, as, gathering her within his enticing embrace he uttered, "Wouldst give thy soul for love of me?" "Yea, even my soul for thy sake" was whispered passionately in reply.

Far down in Berriotdale the midnight bell of Morham Abbey called holy men to prayer and penance; its tongue clappered sharply upon the still air to quiver faint echoes far into the uplands. Floating in they broke upon Issola's ear. She shuddered strangely. Scales fell from off her eyes : and a monstrous terror was begot upon her. Sir Raoul was as a man slain in grievous hard affray with manifold bloody wounds and cuts—his fair face set in the bony hand of Death. With the last wavering note he went from her ; and she fell shrieking to the floor.

Once more the setting moon peered in.

Issola knelt before the shrine, and prayed. Her swollen agony increased. Bowing humbly before the Cross she besought peace for that unshrived soul. " Lord, Lord," she moaned, " have mercy. He was the only son of a widow woman : even of one after Thy Heart's desire. Have mercy, Sweet Jesu, for Thy Lady Mother's sake."

But no calm soothed her troubled soul.

And the moon fell behind the hills; the chapel was again cloaked in darkness; only a beseeching voice broke the silence with yearning prayer.

Her unrest wrought upon her. Clinging

to the feet of the Merciful One, she called piteously upon Him. . . . The ponderous crucifix swayed above her, then fell with a dull thud upon the slim prostrate figure;—a convulsive jerk, a low moan, a few shivers; and the quivering body lay still.

Before dawn a wandering wind blew up from the valleys, and eddying within that silent chapel wove the long yellow hair about Issola's cold face, binding her silken tresses over the great gray eyes that stared starkly upon a lightening east. A spider spun its fragile web, and linked the Cross to the clay. And the elves mourned, for they too had loved her.

The sun arose, and creation awoke. In Duleswater an ancient corpse lay rotting to the air, while screaming kites wheeled above: in Morham Abbey there lay a new cast bier, while sweet incense bore up to God many masses chaunted for a pitiful soul. But beyond the golden bar of Heaven the twain hurried hand in hand towards the throne of the Merciful One.

October, 1894—*November,* 1895.

THE TITHE AT THE MOORSTONE.

THE TITHE AT THE
MOORSTONE.

THE boat was fastened; and I clambered up the broken steps. The silence met me like a friend: no sounds were to be heard, but measured lapping of water against the stone-lined banks, and the occasional cheep of a screech-bat.

I gained the terrace. Nowhere was a light visible: the Grange seemed filled with silence and darkness.

Slowly I wended up the long alley. The beldam, that witch hag, weighed heavily upon my spirits; and a loathesome fear possessed me. In daytime I had brooded over her address and hell-got leer, yet sunshine, and fellowship of men, and ripened wine, had beclogged my apprehensions. Now, walking

betwixt the high, dense hedges of box where
no sound was, for the thick turf as velvet
sunk my footsteps, I was once more affrighted.
Twice had she crossed me, and two times had
evil fortune befallen:—the galleon captured,
my brother slain.

" Egad, man, what of old wives' prattle !"
quoth I to myself; " their gizzards are stuffed
with ancient tales.   Tush ! a fig for the hag's
rubbish!   Did not Bab May last St. Agnes'
Eve tell her beads to my name?   And that
evenly too.   Nay, nay, her malignity cannot
wanton on me!"

But ever and anon as I paced up the
silent, fragrant alley, her words fell back
again; and unwittingly I shuddered.   God
wot courage was a constant companion—yet
affright grew and overwrought me.

My bilbo fastened in a blown branch; and
I stooped to release it.—A torturing scream
broke shrilly upon my ears—an oath—a
scuffle; then silence.

" In God's name what's ado ?" I muttered;
and sped up to the terrace door.   It was
bolted.   This threw me all aback, for never
before had it been so encountered.

Now I heard the west gates thrown open creaking villainously upon their hinges; a clatter of horses' hoofs: then no noise. I ran swiftly round the terrace, leapt the small stream, and hastening up the steep stood upon the margin of the moor. But darkness of night, and softness of verdure, had swallowed up both sight and sound. I turned into the courtyard, and hurried to the wicket gate by the ancient buttery; it swung over to my touch, so speeding through the smaller hall I gained the great staircase.

At the first turn I tripped over a sprawling body—in a trice I was on it, and at the throat. It was a woman. With nervous hands I struck a light; and beheld the countenance of her handmaid.

" Mistress Marion," cried I thickly, "what has happened?"—but she had been stunned by a heavy blow, which yet left a thick, red wealt upon her forehead. So in haste to ascertain the safety of my beloved I caught up the maid, and rushed down the long corridor.

The door of Viola's room stood ajar.

I broke in clamouring her name: but there came no response. The chamber was empty.

I flung down the woman, and with trembling hands lit the flambeaux by the tall mirror : as the light filled the room I noticed full disorder on every side. Viola must have retired to rest ; for her garments with many dainty frills and ravishments of white lay flung aside, while the bed-clothes were betossed.

Hastily I threw water over the damsel's face, and violently shook her.

"Mistress Marion," I shouted loudly in her ear; "where is my Lady?"

She opened her eyes, her lips moved; but I heard no sound. Bending down I caught the low moan: "My Lord! The Tithe at the Moorstone—Sir Jasper—;" and the goodly maid fell afaint again.

This is the Devil's ploy, thought I.

Suddenly the heart sank within me : now, I knew of a certain that an evil eye had been cast upon us. My feet seemed rooted to the oaken floor: aflion was wanting in all my members: I stood as a stucco doll. Meseemed an age passed, and no sounds heard, but sough of the wind through the blighted pines and the dismal hoot of a ranging owl.

It was strange. Fragrance of jessamine still lingered in the room, as it was at even when last we sat in Love's sweet bower. This perturbed my senses with dear recollections: and as a lout, struck dumb with fears indefinite, with bitter grief tearing at my heart-strings, heedlessly I loitered. Then recurred that bodeful wording: "Seek her by the Moorstone when no time is!" and cursing my tardiness I hastened from the chamber.

As I fled along the dark, re-echoing corridors, a mighty blast of wind drave into the house, swirling and screeching through the many passages; then fell a great silence all around. And my heart pat exceedingly within me, for aye on this night did evil fortune befall. From one a babe would be reft, ne'er to be seen again: from another a fair virgin would be ravished—to be discovered next morn lying afield, babbling and disfigured: ofttimes a wedded wench would be lifted from beside her slumbering bridegroom, and next morn at the waking hour a dead corpse chilled his living blood.

All this crushed into my head as unwitting of the way I traversed the outer hall. Its porch stood open; and I marvelled thereat. Neither in my life, nor in my father's, had this been; for time had so rusted and encrusted the iron bratticed halves of the great door that nigh a scoresome of strong men could scarce accomplish the opening thereof: but now, it gaped to the thickening darkness.

I gained the heath. All was still. Behind me lay the Grange buried in the gathering night: beyond—the Moorstone.

I plunged impetuously forward; scudding up the rising grounds like a leveret before pursuit.

Now arose all my grandam had told. This was the eve of witchery's highest revelry—the 30th of April. A great offering was brought this night to the Moorstone; around hearthstones at eventide it was whispered the Evil One himself came and feasted. But no mortal had ever seen and told. Had not my father been found two score years ago on the 1st of May lying in deathly stupor nigh to the Moorstone, his body naked and livid, with impress of great taloned fingers over all : and never again had his voice greeted the ear.

My eager feet sank in a bog, and tardily I set them down again, lest I be pitted and drawn in by the quickening morass. There was no noise, but the swishle of reeds against my body as I bent on. Now and again a moor hen or water-rat was startled, and I heard it scuttle from me. Ever and anon elusive lights shimmered out in the distance to tell of mortals lured to destruction by malicious goblins : and I gathered in my mind, how that travellers crossing between mirk and morning had been lost ; luckless wights snared into depthless morasses.

I broke out into a speedier pace, and prayed the Saints for a stout heart. Haply stumbling into a narrow, westerly track I gained courage with firm ground beneath me. "My God!" I groaned ; "to think of my love in their hellish tricks:"—the blood thickened at that very thought.

As I sped up to the waste land, my brain

pieced together the case,—the heart was with my Mistress.

Yester-even, as she lay in my arms, a cold shiver chilled her gentle frame, and breath failed for the space of a lamb's bleat. As life pulsed back, she clung her tender, soft body to mine; anew the quickening beat of her heart was felt. And sweet caresses calmed the terrified spirit. She wist not the cause, but subtle love caught upon the reason: an evil eye had rested upon her, and thralled.—Ay, and by Sir Jasper had it been cast.

" May God smother him in his own slime!" I muttered thickly; and sped the faster onwards.

At last the dreary highlands were reached. No knowledge had I whereby to gain the centre, where lay the Moorstone within the circle of stone pillars gathered by heathenish hands: I was all uncertain of it. Neither moon nor stars broke the sullen darkness; no stir was in the air. All in a clap, out of the blackness to my right, came a shrill cry of " Help! Help!" Then the silence was broken by shrieks of a tortured being borne far into the night. They beat upon my ear full of a dread terror : and I stood rooted to the spot. Suddenly the air rang with a faint echo of " Geoffrey ! Geoffrey ! " The vague sound died away ; and I heard naught but the pit-pat of my bosom.

Now a harsh, hurtling noise passed overhead ; an echo of discordant laughter and gibberish talk.—Even now were the devilish gang aloose. Already some luckless wight had they fastened upon, and done to death. For this hellish brood was my Mistress to be sacrificed.

A mighty wrath flared up within me, and I pressed on fiercely. Hell's dawn broke red behind a ridge ; some small deer drove rapidly past me : my limbs slackened as timorously I clambered up ; muttering a paternoster the top was reached. The sight therefrom terrified me : by reason of fear my body shook.

Before the Druids' circle, wherein lay the stone, sat a horrid being of evil growth, possessing the voice of man. Around him red columns of fire belched forth beclouding the air with hell's vapours ; far back, until enveloped with the mists of night, grinned

myriads of babbering skulls—ancient witches
and wizards, again to renew the past.   On a
sudden the earth trembled; and I fell quaking
upon the sods.

Methinks I had lain there in stupor a
goodly time, as, when breath crept back, the
space before me was covered with crawling,
flickering flames, and numberless voices filled
the air with hoarse revelry.   My heart gave
a great bound ; but the blood clotted within
its runs : for bound to the Moorstone lay
Viola.   I sank on the turf, riven with unutterable agony.   No prayer issued from
trembling lips—indeed my head was blank.
Then thoughts slowly shaped themselves.
Tradition hath it : that every Walpurgis Eve
the Evil One demands the pure soul of
maidenhood, thereafter to woo it to destruction.   So Sir Jasper, maddened at my felicity,
had outrun all humanity of God and man.
His base malignity roused my beclotted blood;
and I cursed him.   Nay, I could but die
beside her, and balk his devilish intent : and
I started up. . . .

But I was borne upon the grass by an
overmastering hand, that, stiffening all flesh,

turned my body into stone. I lay prostrate, speechless, and mightily afraid.—Verily man is but a beast of the fields, when the spirits of evil and of darkness do stalk abroad.

A voice sounded from among the crawling flames ; as it receded from the circling witchery and drew nigh unto the Evil One, it died away into a long-drawn sob. The person of a male appeared amongst the many, wavering fires; with bowed head and low crouching body he adored : then with indistinct voice he proffered the offering. Great clouds of smoke gathered above as a roof: all sound died away into a deadened silence.

And human utterance issued from the pillar of fire, that, slowly filling the circle, enwrapt the evil growth. " It is good," it said ; " and the soul of the maid is without stain."

Yet there upspake a voice in reverent accents : "Almighty Master, we cast a spell upon her, for she cried on her lover to save." So the bane was recalled : yet the recumbent figure lay motionless.

Forthwith there arose a mighty clamouring of many tongues crying : " A mortal is with us ! "

H

The harsh, unhallowed outcry filled the air; and curling flames shooting out their long tongues sprang upon me from the surface of the earth. My breath hardened—my pulse throbbed not—meseemed I was, and was not. Scant knowledge had I that hell's crowd surged upon me, and surged back again;—baffled. Again they thronged around, endeavouring to devour me: but I was unharmed. Hideous forms filled the air; griffins with hurtling wings and monstrous faces swarmed above, darkening the dim light; huge embodiments of winged snakes swelled up, and spitting at me raged impotently with hellish spleen.

Suddenly like a base chimera the unholy crew went: naught before me but the lurid round of flame and the motionless body of my Love. Yet, on all sides great bodied creatures, mingling with gigantic, wavering shadows, noiselessly massed themselves in the heavens above and upon the face of the sleeping lands. Afar and surrounding the forces of hell were arranging.—My heart went from me: I lay heaped upon the ground.

Now the blast of a mighty hurricane wind was to be heard ; then speeding nearer, and nearer. Many things tossed by me. Yea: the Evil One would snatch me as that thistle-down borne on the gusty breeze. . . . A speck of gold flashed in the red gloomed air, another, and another; then a multitude of small birds with golden plumage and whitened breasts broke over the body of my Love, settling thereon, until she was a mass of wavering gold. The wind caught me. . . .

The grim countenance of night blanched before the oncoming morn ; gray dawn peered upon the mist-swathed hills. I awoke: starting to my feet I gazed with surprise at my strange bed-quarters. 'Twas deuced odd to fall asleep upon the moor. Suddenly the wild fantasy of midnight clappered upon my brain ; and I shivered at mere thought of it.

A scurrying breeze tore asunder the seeth-ing rack in a hollow at my feet. Between the parting shreds was revealed a body upon the Moorstone.

I attained the spot with frantic speed: catching hold of the massive slabs I drew up my cramped figure. Before my eyes lay

Viola, and, upon her swarthy tresses floated
one small golden plume. Through the monstrous enactment of evil God had preserved
her in the hollow of his hand.

Walpurgis Eve, 1896.

THE PASSING OF LILITH.

Toi qui, comme un coup de couteau,
Dans mon cœur plaintif est entrée ;
Toi qui, forte comme un troupeau
De démons, vins, folle et parée,

De mon esprit humilié
Faire son lit et ton demaine ;
—Infâme à qui je suis lié
Comme le forçat a la chaîne

. . . .
. . . . .

BAUDELAIRE.

THE PASSING OF LILITH.

I.

EVENING crept upon the hills. The declining sun fell among golden and purple vapours; the firwoods stood out brown and motionless against a stretch of gilded green ; and the heavens above paled away into an infinity of blue. Soon in the azure west a silver sickle moon would appear to declare our hour of meeting : and I wandered aimlessly about the budding alleys, tarrying until the time appointed.

Verily passion is a cruel tyrant.

God wot no man can restrain himself from the allurements of a delicate woman : and she, unto whom was my heart's domain, had sorely misled me, cloaking with sweet iniquities mine eyes from sin. Ofttimes the soul, that inner consciousness of good and evil, had impelled me unto an higher aim. Alack, I was a weak creature of impulse—will withered under the glamour of her eyes—and at her approach I fell from all reason. Was there ever such sorry slave? Nay! Hotfleshed Faustina wallowing in the reek of Roman harlotry was less despicable than I, for her entire being, bloated with the insolence of domineering desire, unreservedly gave itself up; but mine as a weathervane moved to every motion of an unstable will.

The ancient sage Chrysanthius hath it, that mind is master of the man : certainly he had known no Lais in his youth.

There was an arbour at the end of the myrtle walk ; and thither I turned my steps. A blush rose twining about the trellis-work with matted growth made a little chamber, and scented trails of yellow honeysuckle, disputing the supremacy, clustered about the unfrequented seat. It seemed a wanton act to displace the fragrant occupants; so I strayed onwards meditating deeply upon my egregious folly.

This bondage was a reproach on all manhood; and sickened with past delight, prompted for the liberty of my will, I now resolved for freedom.

Alas! I knew this calm was but a breathing space. Soon my refreshened body would overcome all qualms of comprehension, and, like to a twig of the bitter-sweet the biting of conscience would zest to satiety : reprobation of desire but emboldened and intensified my appetences.

In the train of that last thought came a surge of wanton recollection, probing imagination to the quick. I called up self-mastery : I strove vehemently for self-control.

"I will not seek her to-night" I muttered. "One needs begin sometime :" and high resolution prevailed.

In a neighbouring coppice a nightingale sang with poignant emotion. Soon, passing from earthly strife, it thrilled the song with exalted praise, and cheered my soul.

I plunged burning hands into the cool, gurgling waters of a fountain.

"I shall not go to-night," I cried; and deep determination enforced my feebleness.

A recipient power of restraint passed into the heart; it waxed mighty, battening upon self-conceit. This is an easy matter, thought I to myself—aversion and control are in every man's hands.

And I turned up the juniper walk.

II.

WHAT caused it I know not. — Maybe it was by whisper of the sultry wind, or rich fragrance of the pink mezerion flower, or subtle communication of an all-reaching will; but eager appetence seizing me overbore all opposition.

It grew upon me: until sipping upon the lees of spent desire it intoxicated my entire being.

An impetuous faction possessed me.

Nay! Why ought I mortify my flesh? For paltry pleasure of self-denial—to gloat over such barren virtue and deify myself?—Soul was an idle byword, and inevitable necessity circumscribed us.

Thus did I solace myself.

Alas, this was of frequent occurrence. Of a truth in my calm moments life was a heavy, weary burden; for knowledge of failure embittered, making me less courageous; moreover, the withes of bondage plaiting about an enfeebled brain seemed like to obscure the steady light of reason.

Now sway of luxurious inclination enlarged the empire of my lustihood ; so insistent desire outrunning all bounds drove me thence.

Indeed! 'twas aye a vain dream to deem one moment's victory of avail against her subtle, all-pervading influence.

III.

I HASTENED down the grassy walk, and gained the east postern door.

Upon the inner side of the cope-stone embedded in the high wall was that hideous emblem of fleeting mortality, placed long years ago by a freakish ancestor. Passing out I chanced to look upwards. A malicious leer seemed to flit over the skeleton face with its horrid, empty eyes: and shuddering I hurried with trembling feet from beneath it.

In the firwood solemn calmness of the motionless trees begat quietude within me, stilling the excited senses; and I walked slowly, giving unto the matter a more acute consideration. I pondered deeply upon my unmanly folly. The inner spirit longing for peace and purity reasserted for freedom, yet too weak, faltered in its purpose and therewith failed.

"My God—my God!" I cried hoarsely. "Only to meet Desire as a human being, and grappling, know the worst at once. But to be encumbered lifelong— ": and stretching out vain hands I clutched at empty air.

My heart recognizing its base endurance of desire trembled at the enormity of its committal; yet intemperate madness incited me: and I sped onwards as for a throne.

A dip in the path brought me upon a narrow tongue of moorland. Ancient roots of gnarled heather crawled across the ground, and bade me pick my way with caution.

Now the high tide of revulsion rolling in upon my enervated being swept that shameless delirium of obsession far from me; a great calm obtained sovereignty; and I lingered by the way meting out measure of good and evil.

Strict government of my enfranchized body would demand a heavy, irksome indemnity of my heart—would become the horrid torture of a life, an intolerable anguish—for which was no assuagement but the soothing hand of Death.

And all flesh rebelled from such strenuous denial.

My undirected feet blundered on, striking sorely against the sharp flints and other strewments of the sandy track; but heedless, intent upon this most weighty importance, I overlooked not the way.

Suddenly I woke from my thoughts.

"Nay!" cried I. "Am I to be tost as a puppet ball betwixt my soul and hers?"

So reckless with torment, as malefactor no longer possessing will or body, I assented unto the call of shrieking Pandemos.

IV.

THE muffled roar of sea waves breaking against the rocky headland bade me take heed to the time ; and I quickened my pace.

A gray mist cloaked the marshland that stretched down to the shore.

As I crossed memory of time long-past shot into my head ; and I stood stock-still, so fluttered was I thereby. " Tush, man ! be not a simpleton," quoth I to myself, and took my way again.

Yet a thought grew and over-wrought me, until anger, waxing great, gave short shrift to the delicate vision.

By dallying on the way the night was far spent when at last I approached her dwelling. No lights shone in the ivy-clad pile, save a glimmer in an eastern chamber.

I entered the dark cypress alley leading up to the turret door; the thick grass that floored the winding pathway deadened all sound of approach, and noiselessly I gained the entrance. The iron-studded oak opened

to my touch ; and climbing the narrow stairway with beating heart I reached the top.
Then thrusting aside a heavy curtain I entered
upon the corridor.

Down before her chamber-opening swung
a Venetian lamp glowing with rich colours.
Its scented flames strove to out-illume the
faint light of the new moon, that shining
through high arched windows intermingled
in its sickly beams strange shadows of writhing, clutching, hands.

With scurried flight I made past them.

As my steps rang out in the silence low
voluptuous breathing of a softly piped flute
thrilled the ear, and infused unutterable longing within me.

Like one staggered by strong wine I tarried before the Barolese hanging, nervously
twisting the blue silken tassels with agitated
hands. At length the vertigo passing I softly
entered.

It was a long, narrow chamber bound
around with sweet-smelling sandal-wood,
whereon carved dexterously by cunning hands
were all emblems of the life and death of
Hippostratus.   The ceiling was fretted with

golden fire; and at the further end of the room supported upon the outstretched wings of bronze griffins stood a large porphyry thurible, distilling unnamed odours through the mouths of brazen snakes.

A swart handmaid sat nigh to the blazing fire; and she played rarely upon a flute.

There, soothed asleep, lay Lilith.

He was a wretched wight who gazed upon her alluring countenance: for its silent beauty grew and greatened, until the soul, wavering, was overthrown, and manhood became as a suckling child. Yet I, witless and unheedy, drunk in the appealing glamour with thirsty eyes.

Her oval face was pearly pale, and great sombre eyes lay hid beneath their tender lids, the long lashes closed upon her rounded cheeks. The upper lip of her honied mouth made to bring Life to Death strove down to meet its fellow, one stray lock of golden hair lay curling as a caress upon her fair temples, while beneath the right ear the head of a jewelled bodkin glowed amid short curling hair.

She moved uneasily under my all-devouring gaze.

I pressed my hot lips against her snow-white throat beneath the pouting chin. This amorous theft awoke her. She gave a little startled cry of delight, then laying hands upon my face drew it up, and kissed lingeringly the white, thirsty lips.

"My beloved!" she murmured. "Why did you tarry? My heart misgave me, and I doubted."

The stammering tongue belied my soul; and I clung within her outstretched arms.

She bade the handmaid bring refreshment. That one, turning from us, in short time came back bearing a shallow, gilded maund, and on it small pasties, and fruits, and ruddy flasks of Spanish wines; she also served pale golden citrons, and manchets of fine wheaten bread sweetened with honey; then making an obeisance retired.

"Sabina pipes most excellently upon the flute" said I, advisedly using a modest phrase.

"Yes," Lilith rejoined, "she was taught of me. It is her ear that carries her on—she hath little skill herself."

I picked up the instrument and examined it; its shape was quaint, and singularly em-

I

bossed with strange characters; the mouth-piece, whereon the lips rest, worn and yellow with immemorial usage.

"Time hath passed since that was made" remarked I, laying it down on the cushions. "Ay!" she replied. "'Tis an heirloom made of bone taken from a leman's body : whose charm of music was so exquisite, that she had bereft the senses of all control."

I gave a froward gesture, and bidding her talk of less unholy things poured out a cup of honest wine ; the matured juice quickened my pulse yet steadied the immoderate senses.

Suddenly she cast her deep eyes upon me. Their searching gaze reft from me the striving of my soul. And a strange, unfathomable look crept upon that beautiful face.

Lilith arose: approaching to the fire she stood before the flaming logs.

Daintily she warmed a small, slender foot. The flickering firelight climbed up her shapely figure, touching upon the curve of her waist, glancing upon the sweet occupants of her heaving bosom and the ardent hollow be-tween ; the glittering embroidery enwrought fantastically with seed-pearls and silver upon her clinging gown caught my eyes: and the import of the whole stung my flesh as a burning brand.

Of a sudden she raised her head. "Oh, such gallant lover!" she cried.—"He offers nothing to an hungered one:" and she bowed full featly towards me.

The reproof smote me. Hastening to her I proffered the gilded maund.

"Oh, foolish head!" she whispered, looking down upon me with eyes that set my blood afire—"'Tis the heart that hungers."

I gave no reply: for, swelling with passion, I could but stare greedily upon her face.

"Is it possible you do not love me?" she cried entreatingly; her eyelashes glistening with sudden tears.

"Nay," I replied, "look upon mine eyes. I swear—." "'Tis naught but flattery" she exclaimed petulantly, and dropped her hands in helpless fashion by her sides.

A second passed. My head whirled as a spinning roundabout. I threw myself by her side.

"Let go my hands" she murmured. "You love me not—you love me not."

V.

I LINGERED before the hearth idly watching the blue wisps of smoke. Dawn was at hand, yet darkness overspread the land.

On the fire-tiles was depicted the story of the Judgment of Paris. As I considered that tale the odd fantasy returned, so, immersed in dreamful conjecture I cast me down on a suttee. And lo! as in visions of the night when slumber has fallen I dreamed.

I tarried beside one gowned in pale blue damassin ; and her face was exceeding fair. I wist not who she was—but my soul awoke and leapt up to meet the lovelights of her eyes.

I started ; and gazed stupidly about, until the neighbourhood recalled me.

Now some hidden chord vibrated within me. I was filled with hatred at my surroundings. The air was laden with heavy loathsomeness ; the entire place instinctive of repulsive brutality, and noisomeness.

I shuddered : then a sudden flash lightened my intense brain.

While Death's dear counterfeit had embalmed my senses—by a curious chance, by a whim of Fate's perversity—my vagrom heart had lived, and died, and lived again.

In the wakening sleep of dream Time's pendulum had been tossed far back, misspent years elided, and manhood approved of proper value. Ay! had not my heart once trembled under the sweet tyranny of a woman's eyes, and, under the bountiful influence of that woman's beauty had not mine honour been established? Marguerite! Marguerite!—thy face was the face of my dream.

I sat and took counsel with my soul: and from reason of its sore travail was taught of the wisdom of fools.

But, anew through the sleeping stillness of the house, sweet piping of a flute crept softly.

I started at the sound: it was the leman's flute. Again its amorous strains echoed enticingly; but my heart responded not.

I arose, and stepped to where Lilith slept. In her lap was the pale golden citron with which she had quenched her thirst; its bitter rind torn in several places: between her small round breasts lay a great scarlet lustcup all crushed and withered; one curled petal resting upon that ruddy mouth stained with the kisses of slain youth.

I scanned curiously the sleeper's passive countenance. — My eyes opened; a great horror filled me. Her might was strange and great, nay, deadlier than Death : for he but giveth peace. On whom fastened love for this woman was no rest. For with lust did she lure the soul of man : eating into the core with insatiate appetite she scathed it, until it died. And only in shape did that one remain human.

I had besought God for Desire.—It lay stretched out before me.

A panic gripped me by the heart, and carried away all reason. Bending down I seized one long, black tress. Twisting it about the warm soft throat I had strangled the woman as she lay. Her sombre eyes glared upon me for a second, and I saw therein the lost souls of countless generations. Beneath my throttling hands she died : and the flute was stilled at last.

I fled in madness from the perfumed

chamber : stumbling, twining down the turret stair I gained outer air.

Dawn had lifted over the eastern waves. In the glades the dewy grass glistened with silvern sheen ; and wafts of wind came and went bearing faint fragrance of clover, and wild roses, and meadow sweet. The golden rays of the rising sun shooting through the cold blue heavens chased all shadows from the land.

But I fled homewards through that stilly morning as one accursed—accursed among mankind and brutes.

Lammastide, 1895.

AT THE SIGN OF KYPRIS.

AT THE SIGN OF KYPRIS.

A T last we gained the outskirt of the
woods. The loon's prediction proved
right : at some little distance to the
right stood an hostelry. So Sybilla and I
turned thither with lightened hearts and
eager feet.

This inn was indeed of ancient and rambling
structure; the face of it twisted out of all
shape by the hand of centuries. Huge gables
moss-encrusted and pierced with lattice windows overhung the front, where tangles of
gray ivy and southern creeper smothered the
bulging framework, and hung in festoons
about the huddled chimney stacks upon the
mouldering roof.

By the pale light of the moon the place
had a deserted appearance—there were no

signs of the living. Yet I descried a light
shining in an upper lattice; so lustily wield-
ing the dog's head against the hall door I
rang dull echoes into a still interior.

No heed was given to the noisy summons.
Stepping back I scanned the house. True, no
smoke issued from the gaunt, rude clumps
of chimneys, yet the light was there: so
again I rapped vehemently upon the rusty
platen.

This time, with the desired effect. For
above me a window was opened, and a voice
demanded our wants. I cried we sought food
and lodging for the night, and willingly
would pay any sum for such provision. There
was a murmured assent, and with a noisy
clang the lattice fell to.

"Rudolf," cried Sybilla, closing in to me,
"let us continue on the way. Surely we
cannot be far from Thirlcote? and this place
is little to my liking.—Come;" and there
was a note of lurking entreaty in her voice.
I turned to her with a flourish.

"Madam," quoth I sententiously, "if we
arrive out of the night at the Thirlcote or-
dinary, and stay there—what will the gossips

say over their afternoon Bohee? Depend
on't—the tale will travel to town; and be
marvellously enlarged on the way. But here,
none will know us."

"Oh! I care not, what folks say" she replied, tossing her head; "but the place is
outlandish and strange in appearance."—
"Why!" ejaculated I with affected indigna-
tion. "Surely you can trust to me?"

She was turning with an appeasing reply
upon her lips, when with sounds of much
unchaining the door was unlatched; slowly
it gaped open to the moonlight: and a voice
from the interior bade us enter.

A serving-maid appeared with a light, and
advancing down the long, darksome hall
made speedily towards us. The flickering
flame she bore only served to make more
visible the heavy gloom enshrouding the
entrance, and, when once we stepped within,
the change was as to a sepulchre—the darkness was so great.

Sybilla slipped her arm within mine: and
oddly enough held closer than usual to me;
her skirts rustled against my feet.

Jove, thought I to myself, here's a maid to

clip and buss—as I cast eyes upon the hand-maid, and observed her looks.

She was indeed beautiful. Of middle height and supple form she was a sight for the gods. One might have imagined, her tresses were powdered with dust of golden daffodillies, so rare was the colour. The complexion of the lovely face was delicately fair, and the long silkly lashes of her flashing eyes swept darkling upon the milk-white skin.

She received us with a curtsey, and, announcing our chambers were ready, led way up a great winding staircase at the end of the nether hall.

As we threaded the innumerable corridors and cross passages I could discern on the walls dim faded arras, whereon, enwoven in golden thread, were fabulous monsters of antiquity, Minotaur and his like; while here and there the centaurs strove at the bridal feast.

Suddenly the maid stopped before a door. " You will sup here," she said, glowering intently upon us: then we were ushered into the room.

On the spacious hearth a fir fire crackled and flamed with much show of comfort. A lounge seat was by it ; so with a sigh of relief Sybilla sank wearily into the delicious hollow.

The serving-maid lit the silver sconces upon the walls, and, tarrying ever so slightly by the candles on high mantel, looked searchingly upon the strayed reveller, then sighing wearily, as if of grief oppressed, left us.

" Oh," exclaimed Sybilla, concealing a yawn, " this is better than without. Is it not indeed a quaint place ? See ! " and she pointed round the room.

My eyes followed the motion of her arm ; and I gazed with astonishment about me.

Dark oak panelling lined the chamber, and emblazoned thereon in silver-chrome, all life-size and wondrous fine, was naked Danaë ashowered with glittering gold, Venus entreating love favours of Adonis, and Apollo pursuing with hot feet and eager eyes the faint-hearted Daphne. Again, one saw Venus repulsing Mars, then his triumph over her, while Bacchus strove with a blushing woodland nymph and attained unto his desired

bliss.   At the far end a great oriel was concealed by valenced hangings of purple cloth,
whereon Astarte and her myriad doves were
embroidered in creamy silken woof.

"This is an odd place we have chanced on"
quoth I, turning to my companion.   "Yes,"
replied Sybilla with a roguish look, "I never
thought this forenoon to find myself here.
Indeed, I know not, where I am, but I am
safe:" and she looked up with a smile.

"My dear Lady," answered I, kissing her
hand, "my service, as ever, is at your com-
mand.—Sir Harry Tresham would venture
his Manor and lands to be in my place to-
night."

She laughed. "You are apt to over-reckon
matters" said she, and lapsed into silence.

Now the maid appeared, and, drawing forth
a cover-table made of ebony inlaid with silver
Arabic symbols, set it between us, and put
thereon divers dishes; amongst others, pasties
of peacocks' hearts and tongues of jays.   Con-
fections of candied quinces, and pomegranates
were brought; and ruddy pomewater, and
sugared poperin abed to red rose leaves.
All had a luscious flavour soon cloying the

appetite; so that both but toyed with the dainty fare.

I could scarce keep my eyes from off the serving-wench ; for, clad in a saffron-coloured gown swathled under her bosom with a broad band of golden cloth, she seemed a delicate ramp for a man to deal with. Yet, even as I turned my glance upon Sybilla, I checked the ranging thoughts.

We were served in silence.

After removing all the maid laid malvoisie and almonds upon a side-table by the door.

" Your bedchambers lay ready at this end of the passage " she said as she bade goode-e'en ; "and lights are on the outside." So saying she curtseyed, and retired.

Sybilla inclined to silence, so I reached me a viol lying at hand. It was curiously made and garnished with mother-o'-pearl, the tone quite sweet and clear : so I sang softly Dowland's " Love Meeting."

Then what moved me I wot not : but as in bygone days Azile had sung the love-sweetened ditty, so the tender strains poured from my lips to ring loudly in the room and die away echoing in distant passages.

K

Sybilla awoke from her brown study.

"That song smacks of the love-sick swain, O musician!" cried she. "Wherefore the complaint?"

"I—!" I rejoined. "Oh, no! when in your company there is scant time for the fever to infect one."

"—Or too much" she replied, with a gesture of her head.

I rose and offered her the malvoisie, and having poured out a quantity for myself betook me to the broad settle fronting her.

"Nay, Rudolf! Come here. The seat is ample for two" cried Sybilla, drawing her gown tight about her as I sank into the proffered space.

"There, now!" she exclaimed smiling on me.—"Am I not gracious to-night?" and she blew me a kiss over the brim of the goblet.

"True, this is an unwonted concession" I replied, balancing my silver cup upon the broad shoulder of the seat. "Such a favour has not been granted in all our friendship. "Pray what occasions it.—What do you desire?" I asked in an assumed weary tone.

"—Only the steadfast continuance of your

Don Quixotic service " she answered. " Nay,
unless I exert some feminine wiles, you will
gradually slip away from me ; and once
more I will be lonely in the world."

I laughed protestingly.

She contemplated the amber wine, swil-
ling it slightly about the sides of her goblet.

" My dearest lady," I said lightly, " you
will never be alone : your admirers swell
into a considerable train were the cast drawn
together."

" Ay ! " she replied bitterly. " And what
want they ?—'Tis all their own end. I have
but one true friend " she cried ; and clasped
her warm palm upon mine.

I raised her sweet hand and pressed the
soft white wrist against my lips ; then tip-
ping my cup drank to her prosperity.

Suddenly she raised her deep brown eyes
to mine ; and I saw therein the reflection of
a hidden fear.

" Rudolf ! " said she. " Suppose in life I
fall by the way—what then ? Remember
many traps are set for a woman."

" Ay," interrupted I significantly,—" and
some walk open-eyed into them."

She twitched her hand away from mine.

"You still harp upon the same strain" cried she impatiently. "I tell you—I care nothing for that lean lank of a man. Is that not enough?"

And with an air of bravado she sipped her wine.

"I will even suppose so" quoth I with a shrug: "but in time his stubborn will must overcome yours. Playing with fire is but a game for rogues and fools.—I have been informed you met him at the Rotunda some nights" back I added with hesitation in my voice.

"Oh! Sir Curious knows everything" she flashed out; and lapsed into silence.

For a few seconds I watched her fair sweet face, then bestirred myself.

"Madam," said I gravely, "I am no Sir Benjamin Backbite; but if gossip is rife in the coffee houses with your fair name perforce it thrusts itself into my ears. And you must remember, that the first step of folly severs our friendship—though God knows it will cut me to the heart. I have my probity of honour to preserve. Indeed it is tarnished already by the misconstructions put upon our close and lengthy intimacy." And I rose up from her side.

With a quick movement Sybilla flung herself upon her knees, and seized hold of my hands.

" No, no, Rudolf," she cried hanging upon me, " you must never leave me. You cannot: for you love me."

" Yes," said I with a sigh, " alas, I love you ; and like a fool desire no reward but your advancement and happiness. You are right, my Lady," quoth I with a forced laugh. " I shall never leave you : a man's sincerity of purpose is evinced by his folly."

" Nay, dearest of all! you are not a fool " cried she: " you are the best of men ; and have always advised me to my advantage. I would rather have the 'fool's' word of praise than all the world's. But I am young, and needs flutter my wings : we two can never be man and wife—we would quarrel like dogs in a manger."

" Well," I rejoined, my heart all softer by her affectionate glances, "—see the wings are not devilishly clipped.—Not that I hold marriage according to book and paraphrase necessary for the true union of hearts; yet, the contrary cases are few."

For a few moments she swung our hands to and fro. Then a sudden flush mounted upon her pale exquisite face and stained it a red.

" Rudolf," quoth she softly with downcast head, " I ne'er heard that before from you—'tis a revelation."

" I—Oh, I have held that doctrine for many years, but for evident purposes have never preached it " cried I unconcernedly;—" I had no wish to prompt your belief in it: for at best it is a somewhat pernicious remedy."

Then a new thought struck the addled brains, and shot the hot blood swirling about my heart. With a jerk I stayed her idle swaying of our conjoint palms. At that instant she looked up. But her eyes would not meet my ardent gaze; they fell upon the wainscot to be arrested by Apollo and his fleeting mate: and her colour heightened.

"Rudolf, you are thick-brained" Sybilla murmured lowly; and tried to regain her hands.

A sudden access of passion took me and stormed all restrain. I could not withstand it. Flinging myself at her feet I pressed passionately my mouth against the silvern hem of her garment.

A little laugh slipped from her. She leant forward with a tender look escaping from her eyes. "You may touch my lips" she said simply; and bent her dear face down to me.

II.

SYBILLA had retired to her bedchamber; and I sat alone in the supper-room.

I awoke from my engrossing cogitation as a curious emotion thrilled me from top to toe. I started, and rose to my feet. The candles had long since guttered in their sockets, and save for the fire there was no light.

A strange, languid feeling was in the air. To my eyes it seemed the heathenish deities

again sported amorously with each other:
and the burning whiteness of Danaë's body
perturbed my senses.

Suddenly in the whisht of the house my
quick ear caught the sound of rustling,
falling, garments: then my eyes, as it were,
beheld her lovely, unswathed body—that
body I had so oft enclipt with no thought of
possessing.

The vision scorched my senses with vauncing desire.

Where'er I turned it was the same. The
dazzling sight devoured all reason. And
Venus smiling joyously at the glowing youth
bade him not withhold his cowardly hand.

I strove to banish the arising trend of
luxurious thoughts clustering about my heart
and to demean myself worthily as a man.

In the dim firelight recollections thronged
thickly upon me: once more I was in the
land of golden sunshine and glossy fruit.
Tender eyed Azile, and imperious Julie,
stately Amalie, and love-long Valerie, all
passed before me. With each had I drained
passion to the lees.

Remembrance begat regret of spent pleasures not—not stricken repentance : and alas, I dared to think of that soft form in my loving embrace, and, of my hot persuasion hearkened to by her murmurous dissent. With two hearts beating in unison there could be no wrong : for long years had I loved her : and by her own conduct would I be justified.

Across my memory swept recollection of the perfume of her body as once in a summer gone by I had pressed my ready lips in frolic upon the smooth, firm bosom, where revealed by the mischievous 'kerchief.

This played the firebrand. With a hasty motion I uprose to go—but sank down in the lounge torn with diverse desires.

I buried my face upon the padded arm of the great chair—the chair wherein she had sat. The subtle fragrance of her person yet lingered about the cheveril. Like a callow colt of fifteen I even kissed the spot whereon her arm had rested ; the breath catching in my throat.

I checked my childish outburst.

Good God, thought I, what is affecting me? is it madness—or have I drunk of

Aretinean wine, and am bewitched? What do I intend? And as the base intent flung upon me in its entirety I shuddered at the foul malignity of my purpose.

The flesh justified its existence. What now, O craven heart, it whispered, others have done likewise; even thyself.—What of Valerie, and amorous Julie?

I had no answer for my heart smote me.

"Passion, A Plaything" is the Avenyll motto: and surpassing well had we lived so.

Yet, from the first day of my intimacy with Sybilla, I had struggled for a higher end in view: her peace, her comfort, and happiness. Now it was indeed ironical to have the thorns of the flesh prick the fine bubble of resolution I held professedly in view.

I started up and paced hastily the long room.

In the fitful firelight Mars grappled more violently with the Queen of Love, and Apollo hastened his pursuit of Daphne.

I cowered in the corner and covered my hot, wanton eyes; yet the incitement rampaged about my brain : sweat broke out and poured down my strained brows; and I groaned aloud in my trouble.

But why crucify myself upon the cross of forbearance? — why deny my eager heart that which another would obtain? For the lecherous hound would finally suborn her through sheer predominance of brutal will-power. Sybilla needs give way. And why not when love was in the question, and on each side for the matter o't?

I staggered towards the door distraught with desire and desperate madness.

"And what want they?—'Tis all their own end. I have but one true friend" rang in my ears again; and I seemed to feel her warm soft fingers entwine about my hand.

I stopped short in my steps stricken with amazement; a new reading of my part flashed upon me. "Good God," I cried, "at present I am the worst enemy she can encounter: her betrayal, the repayment for her friendship and affection. Sweetheart, I would be a true friend rather than lover; for the latter goes as the caprice changes, but the former remains for ever. God, God, save me from my evil self."

I crossed to the dying embers and medi-
tated. Honour now spake in brave clear
tones; and I perceived the distinct folly of
my conduct. Sybilla relied implicitly upon
me : she had no prop in the world at large
save me : no kith and kind, nothing but her
dower of wilful beauty and innate sweetness.
So I bowed to the humiliating abnegation
of self.

Weary with self-wrestling and strife I rose
to get abed, and, passing by the oriel, slipped
aside the hangings. The moon had set; a
strange, misty darkness held before the peep
of dawn ; no sounds were to be heard save
the gabble of winging mallards as they sped
northwards. I stirred uneasily as a feeling
of familiarity with my surroundings grew
upon me ; but drowsiness increasing I withdrew.

Without, the corridor was strongly perfumed with odour of burning calambac
wood. The smell caught in my nostrils :
stirring up some indistinct recollections of
times long past it caused me to linger in
the passage.

As I stayed, and, snuffing in the air, tried

to seize upon the particular memories, lo, a light appeared at the far end, and a figure drew into view; so I, inquisitive, stepped back into the darkness of the supper chamber.

The person came nigh: and singular astonishment filled me.

It was the serving-maid.

Naked, bearing aloft a burning golden heart, she passed by; with repulsive horror trailing in the rear. The woman was corporate Life-in-Death. The cruel winter of old age had sorely pillaged her body of its graces—only from the bosom upwards was there the semblance of form. Her shrivelled figure tottered from side to side upon its palsied feet that seemed scarce strong enough to support the meagre, bent trunk and attenuated limbs. Yet her countenance was surpassing beautiful.

She passed slowly onwards; her dark eyes fixed stonily before her, her long silken tresses flashing golden against the loose, bloated skin: and the blazing heart flared upon the horrid sight.

She proceeded lingeringly down the corridor, and brought astand before Sybilla's bedchamber. Full deftly and quietly she opened the door and disappeared within. A monstrous fear laid hold of me ; so fleeing down the oaken floor I stood before the disclosed room.

The unholy hag had advanced to the bedside : her lamp lit up the sleeper, so that I could see the tracery of azure veins upon the side of her near temple.

The beldam seemed confounded : she murmured loudly, and bending over the resting body peered curiously about.

"One," she muttered, "only one !" and her nether lip purled.—"He must be an untoward rogue, for, never before has he unfurnished such goodly gear."

Stretching out a bony hand she made to seize the virgin.

With a mighty effort I shoved myself forward—stumbling on the threshold, to fall headlong into the room. She turned upon me with malignant glare. My tongue clove to the roof of my mouth : move it I could not. Unconsciously my fingers signed the cross, and I fell aswoon on the floor.

Sense came back tardily. At length I

scrambled to my trembling feet and sped to
Sybilla's bedside : she yet slept as if no harm
were nigh. Muttering a prayer for thank-
fulness I flung me upon a settle at her feet
and waited for daybreak.

There were no sounds within the hostelry
—all was silent as the tomb. Now and
again I heard a dry board creak or a rat
scratch at the wainscot, but no more. The
stark silence was so great that it was audible;
yet I cared not, for by me was Sybilla in the
beauty of sleep. I could hear her breathing
soft and low, and by the flickering firelight
could watch her bosom come and go against
the light covering envailing it. No evil
thoughts assailed me; nor did I heed the
darkness that cumbered the land: for was I
not watchman for my beloved in the sanctuary
of her sleeping chamber.

Soon dawn broke over the woods; an
early bird twittered at the window sill; the
gray mist lightened and lifted away. Sybilla
stirred in her sleep: so arising I stepped
gently to her and made to awaken her. She
opened her eyes, and with amazement inquired of my audacious presence.

"We must leave at once" I cried; "I will await on you without." "But"—she interjected. "There is time afterwards for explanations" I declared; and entreated her to hurry.

In a few minutes she was by my side.

"In God's name let us hurry and gain the outside" I exclaimed violently: "this night I have been in Hell."

Sybilla started.

"Your hair is streaked with white" she cried in an incredulous voice. "Rudolf——!" But cutting her short I hurried away.

At last we stood in the great hall. Faint sunbeams straggling through the quarrells cast fantastic shapes and shadows upon the opposite wall; the arras was dimmed with dust; thickened cobwebs draggled upon a floor deep with the mould of many centuries. Yet upon it were the imprints of myriads of footmarks.

We hastened through, and with difficulty unbarred the heavy door.

Sybilla passed out into the sweet air of early morn; her dainty small feet stole softly upon the silent road.

I was stepping over the crumbling flags, when a hoarse cough rang out behind me ; turning round, I beheld the serving-maid. But now she was as the Ancient of Time : lean and wizened were her toothless chaps, coarse locks of grisly gray hair fell in a tangle upon her crooked shoulders.—Her beauty entirely shent.

" We are in great haste " I exclaimed ; and proffered payment.

" 'Tis needless " she replied dully, her leaden eyes blinking to the joyous light of the rising sun.

And again the feeling of familiarity possessed me.

" In former times you rested here " she mumbled ; " and who pays — pays never again."

Amazed at the crone's strange words, as I passed out, I inquired the name of the hostelry.

The hag leered hideously at me : drawing herself up, she cried mightily :—" The Sign of Kypris."

Then the voice weakened ; and the figure drooped.

L

Hidden Witchery.

" I am Passion : true Love hath slain me " she moaned out, behind the closing door.

And I stood pondering upon that saying, until, Sybilla took me by the hand.

Lammastide, 1896.

IN THE HIDDEN HOURS
OF THE NIGHT.

"Fenme ne puet tant amer l'oume con li hom fait le fenme. Car li amors de le fenme est en son oeul, et en son le cateron de sa mamele, et en son l'orteil del pié ; mais li amors de l'oume est ens el cue[r] plantée, dont ele ne puet iscir."

AUCASSIN & NICOLETTE.

IN THE HIDDEN HOURS
OF THE NIGHT.

THE apothecary met me at the entrance. He shook his head. "No," said he in answer to my inquiry, "there is no hope: the end is nigh. She has been calling upon you for the past half-hour" he added.

"Can nothing be done" cried I, as I followed close upon his heels into the unlit hall.

"Nothing," replied he, turning his face upon me: "only the hand of God can save her. The disease has caught upon the heart;—death may come any moment." So saying he led way up a broad staircase leading into a western gallery, and, hurrying to its nether end where glimmered a show of fire, gained the sick-chamber.

Through the half opened door I heard her pleading voice utter my name then die away into an inarticulate sob, as she realized the apparent impossibility of her desire.

For a second I hovered upon the threshold.

Pride battled with my wish to see her : for, with her dishonour had this woman not tarnished my fair name, had she not turned the jibes of the ribble-rabble upon my house ? Then came the low moan—"Rupert, Rupert;" and the sound of catching breath in her throat. Instantly the insolence of my conceit was humbled : and I stepped into the room.

Clarissa lay 'thwartways upon the disordered bed, her fingers clutched tightly upon the clothes. Suddenly she raised herself. "Rupert, Rupert," she uttered thickly; then, with a shrill cry, fell back upon the pillows as a violent spasm shot through her.

I arrested my feet.

Renewed sight of her brought back the past and present : it cauterized cruelly my estranged heart.

Before me lay my wife—the pampered mistress of a dastardly cousin—the notorious courtesan of the town—brought thither to the residence of her paramour to die friendless and alone. And the irony on 't—that I, her husband, whom she had driven to live in foreign lands, should turn in to her by a mere chance as she lay cluttering my name.

The apothecary touched me on the elbow.

"Remember, my lord, this distemper is contagious" he whispered. "Indeed 'tis mighty dangerous to approach ; for the blood, turning acrimonious, has corroded its vessels, and produced pestilential swellings upon the face."

I shrugged my shoulders. "Well," quoth I in a murmur, "betake yourself!"

He shook his head. "Nay," said he, "I will remain until the end. Hear: she calls you."

I nodded as her bleating caught the ear.

In the sombre room the waxen candles spread out a dull and uncertain light; but, even with the indistinct radiation, I could catch an old familiar gesture with the chin as she moved her restless head: a gesture I had noted on her bridal night, as, wakeful with doting love, I had watched her slumbering through the long silent hours.

Suddenly she smote her knees together;

a long low moan broke from her lips as
pain racked her body; then one could hear
the dear breath sucked in between her clenched
teeth.

The apothecary stepped to the bedside;
taking in hand a dish of medicinal waters he
sponged softly her inflamed cheeks and forehead. The ensuing coolness was grateful to
Clarissa. She opened her eyes and weakly
thanked him.

The sound of her voice touched the chords
of memory; it was as clear and melodious
as ever in my time: and I shrank back into
the shadow of the door. As I stood there a
whiff of damp air wafted by me; thick,
musty as of a charnel house: and I shuddered.

Sir Mortimer had no use for this place;
his debauchery swallowed up his rental roll,
so the house was in a lamentable state; a
place more fit for owls and screech-bats than
human habitation.

As the gusts of wind swirled round the
buttresses and outlying gables the windows
clattered loudly against their fixtures; here
and there the lattice-work was broken and
unhinged; so the autumn blasts, bellowing

in, had littered the mouldering floors with
leaves, that lay rotting upon the untrodden
passages. Before me the clouded camlet lining
the upper parts of the sick-chamber was dusty
and torn—one could see the naked wall roped
with twisted cobwebs; while the golden
glory of the embossed leather bordering the
wainscot had faded long ago into a shim-
mering obscurity.

A noise in the gallery made me turn : it
was caused by a female, presumably the
housekeeper, who was mending the fire with
billets of wood. The resinous bulks shot out
a great flare of light, and revealed the most
evil countenance I had ever clapped eyes on.

For a second the woman stood looking
into the flames, then sat down on a settle by the
hearth. Her toothless maw gibbered a little;
she puckered the wrinkled skin of her forehead until it stood beetling upon the pent-
house eyebrows, then suddenly withdrew a
pack of cartes from her empty bosom ; spread-
ing them out upon her lap she contemplated
them.

The logs burned fiercely with increasing
glare ; and upon the discoloured ceiling, with

its fine Italian impasto work all peeling and en-ridged with damp, the shadow of the chimney mantel flickered with leaps and bounds; now covering Herodias as she considered the head of John the First Martyr in its bloody charger, now revealing the Tetrarch as he sat at meat and eyed dancing Salome.

Again and again the crone turned over the devil's books; sometimes wiping her clammy hands upon her tattered gown of betimes rich brocade, but now foully smirched and rent, a mere relic of past glory. She started and shielded her eyes from the glow; then, hastily shuffling her cartes, re-dealt them.

"King, Ace, Queen;—Spades.—Always Spades!" she croaked.

Upon her sick-bed Clarissa tossed from side to side as if to avoid the recurrent stitches of pain; she moaned heavily, then throwing her arms into the air let them fall with a thud upon the bedside.

The crone made a hideous grimace with her in-bent mouth.

"I' faith the poor lamb wants her dearie. Ay, ay, he'll come—there is no doubt on 't!" said she to herself; and turned again to the cartes.

She crouched low against the light, until I could see her twisted shape sharp and black against the blaze.

"Spades,—always Spades,"she repeated ;— "a man with a dagger.—Death." With that there came a hoarse howl of wind about the house ; skirling above the chimney like a gyved fiend. The ancient dropped her cartes in terror upon the flames, and hobbled frantic- ally away into the surrounding darkness.

Yet through the distance I could hear her cry : and the echoing passages took up the call ; it clashed loudly upon my hearing— "Death, Death."

I leant against the wall, for I felt weary and faint : the atmosphere close with must and mould had caught upon my senses ; and my head swam.

The apothecary drew nigh.

" My lord," said he, "it is better, you now go, lest one is met upon whom you have no desire to look—one, who will be here instantly."

" Indeed," said I, " who is he ? "

The man paused. I bade him speak out : he shook his head.

" 'Tis needless to inquire " he rejoined.
" Go your way, my lord, now you have
indulged to the full the detestation for your
unfortunate lady. As you swore, you have
seen her at the ebbtide of life; and what
serves it? "

" But who is the man," I asked, impatiently stamping my foot ;—" Sir Mortimer ? "

He nodded, and looked curiously at me.

I gave a short laugh. " Why man," said
I, " nowadays that fool is nothing to me.
Himself he hurt when he took Clarissa into
his eager arms. Gad! as I know—she was
better to have for a day than a lifetime:"
and I laughed bitterly. " Certes! he must
have been sorely infatuated to regain possession of that poor worn out beauty " added I ;
" but maybe human ware is scarce at present ?"

Then what I deemed curiosity got the
upper hand.

" Does she still care for him?" was my query.

The apothecary scanned me from beneath
his bushy eyebrows; but he did not answer.

I repeated my question.

An odd, pitiful expression passed into his

face. He took me by the arm, and conveyed me to Clarissa, who had fallen into a doze and lay face from us : having dipped his fingers in a dish of camphorated waters, he withdrew from the warm precincts of her bosom a glove.

"My lord !" said he in a low voice, holding up the crumpled and frayed gear into the candle light. "See that ?"

"Certainly," I exclaimed softly. "'Tis a glove."

"Ay! true, only a glove" replied the apothecary; "but the owner of 't:" and he stared me straight in the face.

I thrust forward. My eyes caught upon a silver threaded monogram on the cuff : I started, and seized hold of it.

"Why!" cried I. "'Twas mine years ago. Does she gather such baubles from all her favoured lovers?—'Twill be a pretty stock by this time," quoth I callously ; and, as that thought struck me, I dropped the glove an' it were poison upon the floor.

The apothecary stooped, and having picked up the fawnskin replaced it by her breasts. Clarissa stirred, and awoke. I slipped behind the silk tabby curtain ; yet so that one could observe her.

" Garth," she murmured, " my throat burns. No one is here ? " she queried weakly ; turning her head from side to side as if to espy an onlooker.

The apothecary gave no answer, but handed to her a draught of cooling cordial.

" Garth," she continued as breath came back, " if Sir Mortimer comes hither, I will not see him. Surely he can let me die in peace ? " and she moved her limbs fretfully about.

Garth brought the candles nearer the bedside. " If he comes—he shall not enter here " he said firmly ; " be sure of it : " and he offered persuasively a sleeping potion.

Obedient, like a child, Clarissa took the dram, which obtained an almost immediate effect upon her weakened frame ; her eyes closed, the mouth relaxed its firmness ; with a swoop the minions of sleep bore her thence.

I crept out, and stood over her. For five long years I had not seen her ; yet she had little changed. Of slender figure and exact proportions, she seemed more exquisite and

perfect than ever; her flower-like face, with
the curving eyebrows pencilled darkly against
the pallid skin, more beautiful; but, upon
the low forehead, and about the mouth and
graciously moulded throat, were many cruel
lines of damnatory evidence.

Ay, fairer than ever she lay before me—
the woman, who had crunched my highest
and holiest hopes underneath the heels of
her desires.

Silently I contemplated her.

In her slumber one arm had escaped from
beneath the clothes, and lay lengthways by the
pillow; the fine cambric sleeve was gathered
above the elbow, and betrayed the dainty
shape.

I blinked my eyes. I seized a light, and
bent down. There, just peeping from below
the soft lawn upon her snowy arm, lay twisted
a golden snake studded with purple scarabs
and ruddy jacinths;—the betrothal counter-
change given these seven years back.

I was uplifting the loose hanging sleeve to
obtain inspection, when the apothecary restrained me. "Remember," said he: " you
may incur contagion."

I shook off his hand, and considered the jewelled ornament.

Ay, 'twas the same. There, upon the clasp, were the interwoven letters :—" C : R."

I recovered my balance, and gazed with some curiosity upon her.

Suddenly I looked up.

" 'Tis an odd fancy, that," quoth I, pointing to the bauble upon her arm.

"Ay," replied Garth, " she is very fond of it : to my knowledge, it has not left her arm for many a year."

" Indeed!" I rejoined. " She has not much use now for a pledge of honour, I daresay ; " and I shrugged my shoulders.

Garth cleared his throat. "My lord!" said he. " This is no time to bandy phrases, nor is it my business to meddle with your private affairs, for I am but a serving apothecary : but, of women misjudged—is she ; and yourself is the cause on 't."

I sprang back : the man had touched me on the quick.

" Sir," cried I, " you may keep your clacking tongue to yourself;—as for me, that is my own affair : " and I looked angrily at him.

He clasped his hands nervously together ; his eyes met mine, then dropped ; he wore the aspect of one troubled with a secret.

" Well," said I, in a dry tone, " what has my lord judge, the apothecary, to say to me : " and, somewhat mollified with his abashed attitude, I looked easier upon him.

To my surprise he flung himself at my feet, and catching upon my riding cloak held closely to me.

" Why, man, what tomfoolery is this," I asked sternly.

" My lord, hear me, hear me," he cried. " There would not have lived a purer, sweeter woman than your lady, but for a most monstrous and devilish delusion upon you both.'

I elevated my eyebrows, and turned a cold face upon his rigmarole. " Ay," said I in an undertone, " they all say their purity is tricked away ; 'tis an old song."

Garth pulled me by the cloak. " I swear, it is the truth " he continued vehemently. " In your absence in the Low Countries Sir Mortimer won her away to London upon a pretence ; he forged her letter to you ; he spread the ribald reports upon the town ; he

M

poisoned your ears through the agency of
Lady Betty."—I started and drew the riding
cloak tight about me.—"This once done, and
you absent; friendless, and with bad repute;
with none to help her, what could she do but
succumb to his stubborn, persistent wooing.
Sir! as you know—the flesh is frail; and a
woman is none of the strongest. Forgive
her, sir, ere she dies:" and the man clung
upon my hands.

I disengaged them from his strenuous
grasp.

"What childish prattle is this?" said I
harshly. "You fool—Haines is but one of
many;" and I drew away from the gabbling
idiot.

"My lord," he cried, rising from his knees,
"whom have you ever met?"

"One," replied I sullenly;—"Brittain.
I killed him:" and I laughed brutally,
for the old sore was open all afresh and
torturing.

Garth nodded his head.

"'Tis one," he said slowly: "the other
comes to-night. Sir Rupert," and he stepped
towards me, "have pity upon her. Never,

night and day, has she ceased to love you: and
I swear she has known only these two."—I
gave vent to a spluttering sneer.—" My lord,"
the man pleaded, " what could she do. 'Twas
that—or starvation : for she had no jointure.
You were—God knows where in the South
Seas—and, after young Rintoul's death, she was
penniless, and, for a short time in the Fleet."

" My God!" I exclaimed, as I glanced at
the slim, gracious body and lovely face, and
thought of her lying in that stinking den of
iniquity. And I did not answer ; as, for the
first time, I owned to a sense of my hot
headedness perverted by cruel jealousy.

" Rintoul!" I rejoined at last in a low
voice ;—" what had he to do with the
matter ?"

" He was her friend" was the reply. " The
one person who gave freely his assistance, his
company, and looked for no other reward than
trusted friendship."

"A d——d fool!" I ejaculated: "he should
have ta'en his wages like the others."

" There were no others save the two mentioned " interrupted the apothecary. " The
report she was common property was a

damnable lie propagated by Sir Mortimer to achieve his vile end. She was shunned: she fell. And you—you who should have believed in her—cast her off upon the mere hearsay of a busybody lawyer. My lord, had you come forward, your lady had ne'er suffered nor been misjudged; nor sinned."

I looked at the man : his very vehemence bore a trace of truth : yet I knew he lied like hell.

Bah ! I would trust my perceptions before the sole evidence of a blathering apothecary. She had cozened me from the very hour I first encountered her and her paramour, Sir Mortimer, sitting close in the sycamore room. Moreover, my love was dead, slain through excessive pain of heart and mind.

From the first I had maintained an unswerving aloofness; and that, I would sustain.

Garth watched intently my face.

"Will you not speak to her when she awakes " he implored. " She loves you. See! even in her sleep she clasps your glove to her heart." And in truth she had.

I stepped over, and gazed at her. Her

bosom came and went to the rhythmic beat of her breath, and, between the unlaced yoke, her sweet breasts and tender body could be descried.

An odd feeling crept over me ; a softening of the hardness of my heart : but muttering an oath I faced about.

Then, of a sudden, footsteps were heard in the gallery. Some one swore at the lack of lights. It was Sir Mortimer.

Garth hurried to me. " Now, my lord, the proof is vouchsafed " he whispered. " See —stand in here ; " and he pointed behind the curtains veiling the head of the bed.

I hesitated for a moment: an uncontrolable determination took me ; and I darted into the sheltering obscurity.

Even as I did so, the baronet appeared at the door ; he steadied himself against the jamb, then entered. As he came within the range of light I noted him.

There was no deception about his appearance. One could tell his smooth, hypocritical face among a thousand: his Roman nose with its close-lying nostrils, his cruel, sensual mouth with its thin, compressed lips, were enough evidence of the fellow's character;—gentleman, I had never dubbed him.

Garth met him. " Well," inquired Haines with an oath, "how goes the patient?" and he swayed somewhat drunkenly in his gait.

The apothecary bowed.

" Sir," replied he, "she has fallen into a sweet slumber this half-hour : but I fear there is no hope." The man's voice failed him; he shivered a little, twined his fingers as if assailed with an upstart pain; then, lifting a light from the side-table, lit up the sleeper.

Ho, ho, thought I, here is another victim to her wiles; and indeed it was so.

Haines crossed to Clarissa's bedside.

In the faint radiance of the nightlight one could imagine the puffy swellings upon her pallid cheeks to be the symptoms of healthiness and colour; her lips were parted and showed just a peep of the regular white teeth.

" You must not awaken her " ordered the apothecary. " She is in the influence of a sleeping draught; and dire harm will result if she is disturbed."

Sir Mortimer gave a slight lurch and an imbecile laugh.

"Devil take you!" said he thickly. "Do —do you think I have ridden forty miles to see a pretty face, and no more! She is mine —I pay for her;" and he hiccuped like a stable boy.

"Sir," cried Garth, "if her rest is broken —I will not answer for the consequence. Nay! you must not;" he exclaimed, as Haines put hand upon her.

The baronet swung round with an ugly look upon his inflamed face. "There— there is the door," he growled. "Go!" And he pointed to the exit.

Garth firmly shook his head. "I shall not leave" he declared emphatically. "Well, stay.—But do not interfere in my business" Haines rejoined crossly; then bending down he would have aroused Clarissa.

The apothecary intercepted the descending arm: in a trice he lay prone, senseless upon the floor.

"Damn him!" muttered Haines, as he glanced at the prostrate figure. "She's mine;

every inch of her—illness or none. Bah! a fig for the plague; I'll handle her." And his chops fell as he gloated over the helpless, infected body of his whilom victim.

I peered round the corner of the bedstead.

A fiery detestation for the man flamed up within me by leaps and bounds. I saw before me her traducer—the man, who with devilish cunning and perversion had seduced her mind through stress of circumstance himself arraigned—the man, who had banned my peace of brain and soul, who had filled my ears with vile aspersions by means of his pimpish devices; but above all—he, who had corroded her inborn sweetness and purity.— That brute, with his lanky limbs, and long white hands; the agents of his passions.

I gripped my jaws together; I could feel my lips hard as bars upon my strained mouth; and I stood lurking behind the curtains with hot jealousy pricking at my heart.

I could see Sir Mortimer advance his rapacious hand upon her bosom: with a sudden pluck at the inclosing lace he tore aside the yoke, and fingered her breasts.

The motion and access of cold awoke

Clarissa; she lay staring upon the marauder with dilated eyes; until of a sudden recognizing him she tore herself away. His arms followed fast upon her; they enclipped her: with a lascivious leer on his sallow face he bent down to kiss her.

"Tush, tush, madam!'tis not the first-fruits" he cried, as she thrust her poor face from him; and more lusty than ever he pressed her.

Clarissa struggled frantically to escape his bonds.

In her wrestling the smock slipped from off her shoulders: the upper part of her body lay naked and glowing to the eye.

At sight of this, once my own, a fierce hatred for the man sprang up.—Ay, with the same foul grasp had he not ruined her; tainting her purity with his base desires, with his ramping animal indulgence. But she—! and an unclean reflection darted into my brain to re-heat its virulence against her.

Yet instantly I swerved.

"Rupert, Rupert," rang shrilly in my ears; and Clarissa fought desperately against her keeper.

This woesome bleat for me in her ex-
tremity broke down all barriers : it maddened me beyond control.

Only for an instant did I linger to find my
sword-hilt; the next, I was upon him.

" Unhand her," cried I violently ; and I
hit him on the shoulder with a heavy hand.

Haines dropt her, and leapt furiously upon
me.

Our eyes met. He fell back. His
clenched fists flattened out. Panic-stricken,
he glowered stupidly at me.

In a second I regained my coolness.

" Sir," said I harshly, " you must deal
with me now.—You carrion!" and I smote
him on the cheek.

My sudden appearance had taken both
aback : he glared blankly at me, while
Clarissa lay silent, peering upon me with an
unmeasured look of wonder and uncertainty
in her eyes.

" It seems as if I were unwelcome here,"
cried I ironically ; and bowed towards him.

At the sound of my voice Sir Mortimer's
lips quivered ; his amazed face resumed its
sickly hue ; he recovered his presence of

mind. Then his beady eyes travelled from me to Clarissa, and back.

" Ay," said I, in answer to his thought, "I know you now to be a panderly rogue, a valiant Mohawk—but only amongst women."

" Madam," and I turned quickly to my wife, who lay speechless and wondering, " do you love this man ? "

Clarissa made an idle motion with her lips : but she did not speak, she could but gaze confusedly at me.

I stepped to her. A great wave of pity affected me ; and I took her by the hand.

" Clarissa ! do you love this man ? " I repeated quietly ; looking for the first time in many years into her glorious eyes.

A great rush of blood tided in her, suffusing a ruddy flush upon her pale skin ; her tongue rapped against the roof of her mouth : taken with intermedled surprise and fear she was dumb.

I gently stroked her bare arm. The contact of her naked flesh stirred my tumultuous blood : but I kept a close eye upon Haines.

A second or two passed ; yet she was silent.

"Speak, Clarissa ! Speak. There is nought

to fear " I cried reassuringly. "Do you love
this man?—He owns the preference, then?"
And my tones hardened as certaincy of my
delusion beat in upon me.

She shot her arms into the air. " Before
God and the Holy Angels I hate him " cried
she vehemently ; clapping her hands together
in supplication.

I nodded my head. " Pray, how long has
the hatred existed," inquired I callously.

Clarissa replied not : she but turned her
large, hazel eyes upon me. I started : my
heart gave a great leap : but I restrained myself with an iron hand.

Sir Mortimer moved his feet uneasily
about, then he pulled himself up and coughed.

" Well," said I, coming to him, " what's
your voice in the business—is it that of
Shemei? "—He nervously bit his pomaded
moustache.—" Nay," I continued, "that of
Absalom is more in your line. He plucked
his fruit, and feared to take the consequence."

" See here, bouncer," and I seized him by
the shoulder, " God knows the harm you've
wrought with your lying tongue and starvation tricks, your bawdish feints and instil-

ments : and now the Devil needs have payment on 't all."

"The credit is long o'erdrawn" quoth I facetiously : for I was getting into fine fettle at the prospect of at last killing my man.

Long had I looked for this; and, now he was within my grip, I would delicately slay him. Of t'other question there was no fear : he could never overcome my strength or agility.

Haines moistened his dry lips.

"Sir," said he, "I will make every reparation, but you know "——

I burst into a strident laugh. "Ho, ho," I ejaculated, checking my hollow merriment, "so impurity is to be paid for :" and with a sudden storm of fury I slashed his face with my tasselled gloves.

Uttering an oath he started back and drew his rapier, then attacking, forced me into the light of the candles on the high chimney mantel.

He pinked me sorely in the arm. This disposed of my berseker fit ; and I controlled my movements.

Haines fought from the semi-obscurity of

the shadow cast by the mantel, whilst I was full in the light; but, little by little, I reversed the positions, and began to play with him. Twice I pricked him gently in the ribs as he lounged at me with his clumsy strokes in tierce; and twice, in the sword-arm.

As my guard stood firm he grew enraged: yet it was no avail; I withstood him.

There were no sounds save from the movements of our bodies, and Sir Mortimer's rasping breath. I could hear the Deathhead tick ominously behind the worm-eaten wainscot, and a mouse clitter with its small feet along the leaf-littered floor of the adjoining gallery. There were no lights save two upon the huge mantel overhanging the gaping fireplace, and one upon the side-table by Clarissa's bed. The unsnuffed candles sent out a dim fitful flicker: gloom and darkness enshrouded the room.

A frightened spider scaled his cord as I forced Sir Mortimer against the dusty camlet; and, as he knocked his heels against the panelling, a flock of rats broke away and scurried past the sprawling figure of the apothecary, who lay in a heap upon the creaking boards.

As I drove the long rapier into my opponent's side, behind him on the enwoven cloth
the bloody nail of Heber's spouse seemed
redder than ever; more ruddy, than his life-
dew upon my fleckered steel.

Haines thrust wildly at me. In vain. Again
and again I pierced him where I willed;
puncturing his fine brocade waistcoat and
Hollands shirt into bloody patterns of revenge.

All honour went from me. In a furious
lust of vindictiveness I drove my pointed
blade deep into his shrinking body. I
shouted with glee as I felt the steel slide in.
Bah! why should I treat him with honour
who had perverted my wife's—his was rotten
at the best, rotten with debauchery;—and
these arms had constrained Clarissa, had
compelled her to dishonour or starvation.—
And I circled round the doomed ravisher,
plying my steel in his rank flesh as a house-
wife her needle in the sock.

Sir Mortimer became weak; he clutched
at the wallcloth to sustain himself. With a
noisy rip the decayed stuff gave way; and
bellowing, he fell on me. I stepped back:

with a dull thud he landed above the body of the apothecary, and, stunned, lay motionless.

An irritable sense of deprivation moved me;—I would he had given more sport: and with a kick I turned over his carcase to view him;—him, God's Image!

But, with that, there came a moan from Clarissa who now wrestled with Death, for, alas, the hot, pestilential fever was encroaching close about her heart.

I advanced to her with combative fury and hatred yet swelling upon my lineaments. She looked at me as I were the Basilisk. Then her fearful eyes dropt upon the dripping rapier : with a scream, she covered them with her hands.

Cursing I threw it from me, and laughed harshly.

"Madam!" cried I hoarsely. "See the cause:" and I pointed to her fallen paramour.

She gave a little gasp as her glance alit upon him ; her fingers crept upon the open smock, and tore at the Brussels lace edging the yoke ; the blood fled from her flower-like face, leaving her mouth a scarlet ; her heavy underlip quivered. Suddenly she raised her

beautiful eyes to mine, swiftly to let them
fall again. Her glance but clung upon my
face for a second : yet I read therein her
passionate appeal.

Her great eyes made a flare of my
doubts, consuming all indifference, all in-
action. The innate purity of her heart peered
from their lustrous depths ; and the thrill of
its desire, entering anew into me, trumpeted
the retreat of wavering sophistry.

" Clarissa," I cried, with my soul clamouring on my lips. " Say: it was not wantonness ? "

A look of intense agony blanched her
face ; she shut her eyes : but I got no reply.
Tears glistened underneath the dark, silky
eyelashes, to roll down her wan cheeks ; her
bosom heaved with short, convulsive breathing ; she stretched out her groping hands
to me.

With a great sob, I threw myself upon the
bed, and covered my face with her small, hot
palms.

" Hush," she murmured, as I sobbed out
my shame, "mine is the blame. But you
were cruel, Rupert—oh, so cruel : " and
breath failed her dear lips.

N

For a little time she did not move. I looked up: she lay back upon the pillows with no sign of life, except the twitching of her mouth.

The apothecary was right.

Haines' rude awakening of her had augmented the misordered spirits; and she was dying: dying, alas, too soon for me repentant; dying by reason of him, with his damned intrigues and brutish lusts. Death was at hand to carry away her rare beauty and goodly heritage of body, whose singular fairness had occasioned the marvellous cruelty of her lot: and I, rendered dumb by the tumult of my senses, stood heart-stricken above my regained love.

In the deep stillness, my ears caught the stirring of Sir Mortimer. In a trice, my hatred and loathing for the man seized possession of my mind: and a devilish subtilty was invented.

I turned to the man—he yet lived. With rough handling I trailed him across the room, and set him on a tall-backed chair by the top end of the bed.

Haines recovered somewhat, and, rising up, endeavoured to walk. With a pounce I was upon him ; binding a rent curtain about him, I had him stiff and certain as a mummy of the Pharaohs.

" Curse you," quoth he faintly, " what play is this ?" as I bound him faster and faster to the seat.

" You see her ?" said I, indicating the faint image of Clarissa in the tarnished mirror fronting us.

He nodded sullenly.

" Well," continued I, so softly and gently, " she is dying—dying because of you ; " and my voice sank into silence.

Then I struck his lying mouth.

" Ay ! " cried I fiercely.—" It shall be blood for blood—life for life."

The baronet's face whitened. " Why," whined he, " what is 't you mean ? "

I smiled fiendishly at him, and, having whipped out my hanger, cut up his gray cloth sleeves. He swore and twisted about ; but an idea occurred, so pulling his jaws asunder I gagged him with his own silk handkerchief.

Thereupon, I stepped back, and contem-plated him in the dim candle light ;—the

craven was now writ plain upon his countenance.—But I, to my business.

Hanger in hand I stood behind him. As
a surgeon, I fingered his upper arms, then,
laying the cold, sharp blade against his soft,
yielding flesh, I ripped them upwards, most
dextrously, from the elbows.

Thus, I treated the ravisher of her honour.
And I could feel him cringe beneath the
knife.

I bowed to him.

" So," cried I, " is flesh rendered for flesh : "
and, as I went from him, his blood bespattered
the floor.

As I traversed the chamber the physician
gave a gasp, and drew his body together ;
rearing himself upon his elbow, he gazed
dazedly around. I assisted him to his feet.
He staggered towards Clarissa : seeing her
afaint, he motioned me to sprinkle upon her
face some waters from a phial he carried about
his person.

This revived her ; and life again flickered
upon the beautiful face.

She felt about for my hand, then carried it
to her lips, but, too weak, needs let it fall.

The apothecary put his cold fingers upon my hot sword-arm : they chilled me to the bone. " Sir," said he, " Death will come in the twinkling of an eye. See to it—that you acquit her."

My head bowed upon my bosom.

" 'Tis I," I replied lowly, " who sue for remission ; for I am the true culprit. My hotheadedness and weak belief did forward her ruinous descent : she had none to help her."

His grasp tightened upon my shoulder-blade, till I winced. " She will have strong cordials to retain animation for a little while " he replied. " Sir! Forgive : as you will be forgiven." Turning to her, he administered the retarding draught.

And in the stillness I heard a drop, dropping upon the floor.

But there came a weak cry of " Rupert, Rupert."

This tugged at my heartstrings. Long pent passion, bursting up, broke all bands of foolish scruples. She called on me—Clarissa, my first and only love—and straightway she was in my arms.

For long years had I thirsted to feel the touch of her gracious body, the music of her soft voice, the fragrance of her hair : and, half mad with joy and grief, I clipped her to me. What cared I, although the malversations of brutes had besmirched her corporeal qualities—I owned the empiry of her heart and brain.

Clarissa lay in my arms, her queenly head upon my bosom ; with a contented sigh she clung close to me, her eyes fixed steadfast on mine.

" Dearest of all," she whispered, " I am happy at last. I knew you would come to me. Oh, Rupert!" and she kissed the braiding upon my coat.

" Hark!" she ejaculated faintly. " What is that?" and she thrilled strangely, as the noise of a drip-dripping echoed in the room.

I laughed nervously. " 'Tis the ivy without " I answered softly ; and caressingly reassured her. But I glanced aside uneasily, as the sound grew louder.

" Hear! 'tis again " Clarissa murmured.

" Hush! it is some one walking in the corridor " I replied ; and stilled her fears.

The fever returned, and wrought upon her senses; she babbled of childhood and early years.

Suddenly she threw herself from my hold, again upon the pillows.

" See—there he is "—and she pointed into a dark corner.—"Ay, he's coming—coming. Rupert!—Save me—save me : " and with a scream she buried her face against me.

" Dearest," cried I, all astagger, " there are none here save Garth and I ; " and gently stroking the hot, beating head I strove to calm her.

But, upon the tabby curtain, grew a large, irregular stain. Slowly it deepened into crimson hue, as the gore, clotting upon Sir Mortimer's dripping elbows, soaked through the silken woof.

I looked furtively about for the apothe-cary : he was nowhere to be seen. There was a loathly stillness about the place : within, without the house. There was not the merest shimmer of fire in the corridor : the open door of the bedchamber seemed a sheet of blackness. In the room the gut-tering candles wavered with sickly shoots of light; mere embroideries upon the inclosing gloom.

Clarissa slowly turned her face up to me; her eyelids contraćted; she shivered.

" Rupert, Rupert, who is coming near," was whispered hoarsely : " oh, it is so cold." Then she opened wide her eyes. " I see him! There is his cruel face, and grasping hands.—Ah." With a piercing shriek she fell heavily against me.

And the gory splatch grew, and greatened upon the creamy silk.

The atmosphere became more chilly and stagnant; an odd feeling affećted me; a tremour caused my jaws to chitter as in time of frost. I held Clarissa closer to me; stubbornly, as if one was by me to reft her away : and shouted upon Garth. But he came not.

As my look at the door sped back to my beloved's face it traversed the mirror opposite me; simultaneously, the flames of the expiring candles gave a few leaps, and the room was nigh filled with night: ere that—once more, my eyes had beheld Sir Mortimer. His head had fallen upon the left shoulder; his nether jaw hung loosely down: but his dimming sight was fixed immutably upon the reflecting surface.

Casting a silent curse in the waning gaze, he stared at us with his protrusive, bloodshot eyes.

With a hiss the lights were drowned in their fat: but, in the faint light from the floating wick by the bed, the ruddy stain seemed shapened like a bloody hand fastening upon Clarissa.

She moved. "Kiss me, Rupert," she murmured. "Oh, I am tired, so tired:" and feebly she nestled in to me.

Not one but a thousand kisses did I rain upon her sweet lips and face. Thought of her cruel lot and pressing death fairly broke me: and I wept over her; blubbering like a child.

"Ladybird, ladybird," I sobbed. "Would God, I could die with you. To find and lose you so soon." And I ceased from the intensity of my grief.

Behind the tabby, I heard the death-rattle richochet in his gurgling throat. His head struck the back of the chair. And a speaking stillness followed on. Yet, there sounded through the silence, that drip-drop, drip-drop-dropping upon the floor.

Clarissa uttered a moan; her clasp tightened about my neck. I gently placed the bed-covering around her. Suddenly she sat upright. The night-light flared up. Her eyes caught upon the monstrous sight beside her. She started, and tore aside the hangings . . .

Her face stiffened with fright; for the moment, she held her breath. Then, with a shrill laugh, she fell upon my neck, and died.

. . . The slow hours passed by. Alone, with the dear dead in my arms, I stood void of all sense by reason of unutterable agony. Not until milch kine had lowed in their stalls did I move: then with a sigh I stroked her dark tresses; and, holding her closer to me, I bore her silently away—anywhere, anywhere, away from his accursed vicinity.

Martinmas, 1895-1896.

AT THE CROSSROADS ON
THE MOOR

AT THE CROSSROADS ON
THE MOOR.

THE wind moaned without the Grange. Now and again, coming in great claps it swirled around the gables, and cried with strange and mournful notes in the darkness. All was peace and quietness within the house : the household had retired to rest ; and, save the steward who awaited my departure, Yssolane and I were alone.

Into the ear of silence struck the hour of eleven. With a start I rose from my beloved's side.

" Jove," I cried, " so late already ?—and I, here ! Why, 'twas my intention to have left ere now : for much must be done before I get abed : " and, stepping to the little rose window, I drew aside its silver-threaded tappet, and considered the night.

"Egad, it is dark," quoth I, as the blackness loomed in, and filled the window frame as with an ebony slab. "Hear to the wind!—it moans to-night, as if the devil and his angels were abroad:" and I gave a laugh.

She drew close to me. "Nay, dearest, do not go," she cried beseechingly, as rain bespattered the pane. "'Twill be a stormy night. There's no cause on't. Stay, Ralph, stay by me; and leave in early morning!"

I turned from the threatening darkness to her fair beauty.

"Sweetheart, sweetheart!" I replied. "What would gossips say? How their tongues would wag! 'Twould give Mistress Harkaway a month's talk. Oh, the scandal of it all! Fie! Fie!" and I pulled a pretentious face.

Yssolane playfully smote my lips with her forefinger, and reiterated her plea. I shook my head, and, catching her in my arms, carried her to the fire; setting her down in the ingle-neuk. I resumed my place beside her on the cushioned settle. Her countenance brightened, and testified to her belief of my intention.

" Nay, dearest," said I, in reply to the tacit
testimony of her glancing eyes : "I must away;
for the day after to-morrow sees us wedded ;
and I have attended to little or nothing.
When the candles gutter; then I'll off.
Moreover, 'tis only some six miles home ! "

I plied my case with all cogency; yet
she gave no ear, but plead the more beseechingly.

Now, as if to reinforce her argument, the
wind increased, and, growling around the
chimney stack, stirred the dying embers into
a lambent glow ; the rain shivered with force
upon the lattice panes ; and, in the courtyard,
the gargoyles gurgled and spouted with in-
cessant and louder splashings. Her dear
company and cheery chamber did indeed
retain me ; but, at the guttering of the candles,
I arose, and made ready to depart ; though, I
own, with much self-compulsion.

As I fastened my cloak tight about me
Yssolane again plead strongly against my
set purpose.

Some hidden fear seemed to lurk within
her. She clung to me as if to retain me with
her gentle hands ; and, words failing her, lay

upon my bosom with strenuous entreaty writ large upon her eyes.

"Dearest of women," I cried, "have no fear. Blindfolded, Cassandra and I could cover the road : if one fails the other will surely travel home."

With sweet reassurance I strengthened her uneasy mind ; and, loosing me from her arms, stepped out into the darkness.

On the face of it, the weather seemed more ominous than stormy. Through the flying scud in the sky one could detect the faint starlight ; down in the east, over the rugged hunch of Dead Man's Law, blinked the peaked face of a new-born moon, swathed between woolly bands of mist : yet a feeling of something impending was in the air ; and for a moment I remained swithering on the doorsteps.

"Bide ye where ye be, sir," cried the steward, as he held the stirrup : "'twill be a wild night. Bide ye where ye be : 'tis Easter-tide !"

"Tush!—a bag of wind, and a dish of rain" I replied, making for the saddle. "And what of Easter-tide?" Jaggard shook his head.

"A bad night to travel on, sir," he answered. "The dead arise to seek redemption; and the Fiend claims his own. God forfend the right!"

"A list of packman's lies" quoth I. "Good-night!" and, with a nod, I rode off.

A few roods away, I turned round.

There in the west window of the bookroom, a great flare of candles in her hands, my beloved stood, vainly striving to discover me. As I looked the steward approached; took the lights from her; the twain disappeared into the hall: and nought remained except the blackness, and the driving wind and rain.

With a shiver, I rode onward into the blustering night, but ever and anon turned again, as if that dear scene yet greeted my vision.

When well on the road I repented of the outset. The wind blew snell; coming with impetuous gusts, it battled about me and shook the sure-footed mare from her foothold: the rain increased, it cut against my face; soon to penetrate my clothes and chill me to the bone.

Marry, thought I, it is little wonder Yssolane had bodings, as Cassandra rolled from side to side and stumbled on in the now

o

thickening darkness; for hurrying clouds had cloaked both moon and stars. The wind swept across the hill-land, howling like Beelzebub; the rain lashed against me with sharpened force: and I had much ado to keep my seat, far less note the way.

Thinking to obtain a sheltered path, I turned off the roadway into a bosky bottom that wound to the moor, down to the cross-roads, where the hill-track converged with the highways.

As I rode down this hollow the air became more stilly; though above, the storm yet ripped shrilly across the gap. In time the wind grew calm, and the rain ceased save for a spent spitter. Around me the trees stood together thickly—I could scarce see to pick my way beneath their overhanging boughs. The darkness deepened, and the stillness greatened: never a stir in the wood, never a motion in the air; no sounds around me save the crackling of withered branches beneath Cassandra's trampling, or the occasional hoot of an adventurous night fowl.

I had gone some miles, by this; and now heartily wished the journey at an end: my travelling so lonesome and eerie. 'Twas as Nature were dead, or collecting her forces for some monstrous outburst.

Some little way on the wood thinned apace; but this did not lighten the murky gloom, that settled down and packed the intervening spaces.

Suddenly I pricked my ears, and drew Cassandra a-standstill.

A strange sound shivered the silence : around, afar and anear, a rustling murmur filled the air. The heart of the wood thrilled with mysterious fears ; the leaves began to sharpen one against another with sibillant agitation. Then quietness reigned. A stoat scuttled, from out a coppice, squealing with alarm : it dashed against the horse's hoof ; only to flee onward squealing louder than afore. Cassandra took sudden fright, and bolted from the spot.

I regained the mastery with difficulty ; and we jogged onward at a speedy pace.

Soon the mouth of the bottom was reached. And, with a sigh of satisfaction, I noted the gloom lift somewhat ; due, doubtless, to a rising breeze that came and went in puffs.

I neared the turn whence the path debouched upon the crossroads. Cassandra slackened her pace. Suddenly she stopped —move she would not, but stood stock-still with splayed feet and labouring nostrils ; a shiver throughout her frame.

Some strange affair must be ago here thought I : and with that got off her ; and going ahead some few feet peered inquisitively about.

Nought could be descried among the bracken and broom : nought save the darkness which seemed to fluctuate and waver before my very eyes.

" Pest, upon the night ! " cried I. " One could think Satan moved all nature to his hand ! "

Even with that a bellow of wind blustered down the bottom, screeching and weeping like very hell's self—Cassandra broke from me. Turning in a trice, she fled up the way we came, neighing like a steed demoniac.

I burst into a volley of oaths, and took after the galloping horse: but in vain ; already the beat of hoofs was dying away in the distance.

" Lackaday," I cried, " it will scurry back to the Grange : and then, such hubbub as man never knew ! " and I fell a-swearing like a Spanish Walloon.

However the fit of anger spent I set homeward ; for though the moor road was lonely yet it was fine, firm walking—whereas the path Grangeward was full of many woes for a benighted traveller ; and I own to little liking for the woody part, 'twas so eldritch. Moreover, the stretch was only of some three miles more : and I was at my gates.

Now the wind had arisen, yet, as the rain held off and the road ran free, I stepped out merrily. But in a few minutes the song died upon my lips ; the lightness, from my heart. The soughing of the wind as it moaned around the broomy knowes appealed to some dread sense within me, and instilled a certain sensation of fear, foreign to my nature.

I closed my ears to the eerie sounds, and forced my pace ; but aye the breeze seemed fraught with a strange burden.

The moor lay still ; never so much as rabbit's spud, or curlew's call. And as I neared the crossroads remembrance flashed into my head of the dead lying there:—an Ægyptian slain by her own hand ;—buried in a suicide's grave, her body impaled by a stake through the bowels.

I shuddered, and, by closing my eyes, tried to drive away the recollection of an ashen pale face and ruddy-ringed throat.

Of a sudden a motion of fear shot into me.

With a start I gazed before me. I blinked my eyes. I closed them; and threw my hands on my brows, and wondered if I were dreaming. On the patch of ground that knit together the roads was an illumination of tapers—the figure of a corpse—the person of a man.

I had never deemed myself a coward ; yet now found myself on my hands and knees; hiding from that light as a thief in the night. Who the man was—who the corpse—I knew not. An uncontrollable shuddering rippled into me ; a desire for instant retreat : but with a muttered oath, cursing myself for my cowardice, I advanced warily upon the scene.

But, mark you, some instinct ruling me, I

crawled and crept like the vilest spy in creation,—which is far from my nature.

At length I came within some three or four ells, and covertly ensconced myself upon the near side, behind a great bush of eldergrowth.

'Twas the corpse of the suicide : I could note her swarthy tresses clotting to the decayed head. The body lay stretched East and West; the arms by the sides. The putrified hands bore altar candles; the feet, likewise : and strange, though the wind swayed the eldergrowth, the flames never flickered but unwavering shed their light; I could note the stuff that bound the tapers— 'twas silken.

The Man, his face was from me; I knew him not: yet, by his hunchback, now could tell him amid a thousand.

He contemplated the loathsome spectacle for a moment: then, with a gesture, placed a sacred wafer upon the liquid lips; and on the swimming eye-balls. With his hands he made three mystic signs, and three times three walked round the body.

I strained my sight to observe his face, but alack, it was so swathed with linen, that nought was visible except the eye holes in the spotless bands.

Then the import of the whole broke in upon me. At Eastertide witchery renew the instruments wherewith to work their evil will. And the Man sought an unshrived soul : striving with the subtle wiles of Hell to conjure it from its dread abode by false hopes of redemption from sin and probatory punishment. Thus he wrought to secure him his familiar for a term and a term.

The dreadful significance cruelly clouted my brain; a cold sweat gathered on me; I lay crouching behind my shelter, sapless and inert.

At the ninth round the Man tarried before the Ægyptian's head. He made an abominable obeisance towards the East; then removed the wafers, and spat blasphemously upon them.

A hurricane wind clamoured around : yet never the lights so much as flickered : they pointed steadily upward as if to pierce the louring clouds and attract the eye of Heaven. But the darkness deepened, swath upon swath.

The Man stooped.   Taking a golden

chalice in his right hand, he sprinkled holy wine upon the mouldering mouth and fore-head; then made three mystic signs; and three times three walked round the dead.

But I had no thoughts on him. Out of the night I saw a vast Shadow loom and overspread the land, covering heath and home: till with encircling closure it surged in, and in, upon the unhallowed spot. Yet the Man knew it not.

Again at the ninth round He tarried before the Ægyptian's head: once more to spill the holy wine of redemption upon those accursed lips.

The Shadow came nigh. Within its cloak of chilly blackness my horror-stricken eyes descried the hideous forms of Hell's prisoners: crowding, crushing to its lessening rim, to wager on Hell's Plot against High Heaven. And the Man knew, and bowed before the shadow: and, crying with a loud voice, com-manded the unshrived soul to come forth.

The corpse quivered: it thrilled; and was transfigured with life.

The Man arose, and smote the woman heavily on her mouth with the crucifix.

The doors of death swung open: and the tongue of the dead was loosened.

An overwhelming outburst of terror rioted in me. With a mighty effort I found a voice. "Dear Jesu deliver me" rang from my very soul. But the boom of the startled bitterns drowned my cry: and the Shadow still came nigh. . . .

When sensibility returned a morning sun poured his glory upon the moors; the air was balmy and pellucid; no clouds fretted the serenity of the blue sky.

I sprang up, and looked about. My eyes bore upon the crossroads; and without interest: the Man—it was the Man—I looked for; and though no trace of the affair was visible I fled in mad terror from the spot. The sun, the freshened air, the springy turf soothed my troubled brain; and my heart lightening, I clapped my hands in glee and shouted with delight.

Ere I knew I was beside a cot, around which a scattered band of men was collecting. I stood stock-still. Fright paralyzed me: the Man might be there. But in an instant I was off. Voices cried out my name.

'Twas but a feint of His: and with a cry of dread I sped the faster.

I heard the sound of runners; of pursuers: their calls to one another; their nearing feet. I redoubled frantically my pace: a false step —a shelving bank; and I fell headlong into a bushy thicket.

The pursuers plucked me out with tender care.

"The Man! The Man!" I yammered; and thrust violently from them. But firm hands held me, and strong arms wound about.

"Who, master, who be the Man?" my servants implored. I but gibbered the faster, and struggled the more. With sorrowing and wondering hearts they bent homeward, carrying me in their arms.

Midway, across a swamp, they encountered an early traveller.

"Why, what fool is this?" cried an arrogant voice, as I lay babbling and foaming at the mouth. "The Man!" repeated the horseman: "what Man? Let me see the idiot. Lackaday, — Sir Lovelace! Woe woe,—'tis a mournful sight for his bride!"

Affright seized me. I stopped my babbering ; for a moment, the tongue clove to
the roof of my mouth.

"The Man, the Man," I cried shrilly ;
and, pointing at him, wrestled violently with
my keepers.

"God's life, he is moonstruck ! " said the
rider. " How he froths and fumes ! Stand
aside, loon : " and he jerked his bridle-rein.

" Nay, nay, not so fast away !" called a
voice. " Confront him with the master.
Maybe he can say more." And willy-nilly
they dragged him to me.

I shrieked, and strove to escape ; but all
anought. They confronted us. His hunchback seared my sight like a red-hot iron. In
a fit of bedazing terror I spat at him.

" He hath bewitched the master," cried
one. " Ay," echoed another : " sink or swim
the wizard in the moss."

So in a tumult of cries and strife they tossed
the Man far into the quickening morass.

He crawled to the side;—only to be thrown
farther into the slime. Again he floundered
to the brink. With their swords they thrust
his bleeding carcass deep into the sludge.

Now I lay quiet in the grip of my keepers, crowing with delight, and, loosened, could do nought but jump, and jump, and hulloa from very joy.

A strange Shadow fell athwart the swamp as the Man sank low, and lower, into the slime. His evil eyes hurled maledictions upon us; but never spake he a word. And the Shadow flitted nearer and nearer to his head.

Deeper and deeper he dropped. The swelling slough swayed around, heaving to his maddened struggles up against his chin.

With a gulp he disappeared beneath the surface. As his breath-bubbles welled out on the quivering ooze a burst of fiendish laughter grated from above: and I stotted to the ground, raving like one demented. . . .

The murmur of a cushat call floated in through an open window; it sounded sweet in the dewy gloaming; filtering in, with the odour of blossom and garden scents. Without I saw some fir trees dark and high against the pale blue evening sky, and through my half-closed eyes looked at the crows hovering about the bushy tops. Ay, said my wandering thought to my fevered brain, I'll harry the nests to-morrow—if my mother's not at hand: and with that I fell asleep.

When next I awoke it was daytime. The curious sun slipped in his beams between the shaded lattice. One ray glowed across the darkened chamber, to fall upon a *prie-dieu* encumbered with the gown of a kneeling figure.

I gazed vaguely at this sight for some minutes. The sound of weeping fell upon my ear, and roused my heart from its dull repose. I started up, but fell back with a moan. "Yssolane, Yssolane," rang from feeble lips.

Then quick, soft patter of flying feet: a wet cheek on mine: and heart spake to heart again.

Eastertide, 1897.

THE POTION,

OR,

THE TRAGICAL ENDING OF THE LOVES
OF VIOLA, DUCHESS OF SIENA, AND
MARZIO, SEIGNEUR D'ALIBERT,
HER SOMETIME LOVER.

. . . It fell upon Martinmas Eve that this marvellous beauty died : some say of the same poison, which, all unknowingly, she had administered to her lover ; yet some say otherwise ; averring her death was occasioned by the Fearful Hand of God. For as the fair and carnal Lucrece, daughter of the Borgia, nourished nought but foulest leprosy of sin, so this, the prodigious beauty of the time, nourished nought save cunning murder and lewd wantonness of body. Therefore, her sudden death, the multitude assigned to Divine Retribution. Truth to tell, upon beholding the monstrous destruction of her lover, she died as a common woman ; of a broken heart. . . .

ISLIP.—*His Journey.*

THE POTION.

An hour before midnight. A large, square room on the topmost storey of the west donjon of a castle in the Apennines. To the left, there is the staircase door: to the right, a door opening upon the battlements of the tower. The stone walls of the room are dusty and bare, save beside the three, narrow, upright windows, where hang dark, heavy curtains of coarse cloth. The east window is uncovered: through the chinks of the shutters comes a low rhythm of dance music, borne upon the gusty wind; now and again raindrops sweep heavily against the wood. Most of the room is in shadow: sometimes, from the fires and furnaces ranged against the walls, dull red flames leap up, and fill the darksome place with a lurid glow. Upon the north wall hangs a lamp; the body thereof, a human skull

P

ribbed with silver bands. From it a long tapering flame is emitted, which shows up indistinctly the copper alembics and other appurtenances of the alchemist, who sits beneath the light alongside a narrow oaken table, upon which stand a few phials and an hour-glass. He reads a manuscript. There are no sounds in the room, save the music faintly intermitting as the wind comes and goes, save the bubbling of liquids in retorts and pans.

The ALCHEMIST *folds up the manuscript. He turns the hour-glass.*

ALCHEMIST.

'Tis yet three minutes to the appointed hour. That is—by the method of infusion Malabris used. (*He opens the manuscript again, and reads.*) "When the golden liquid clearing, becomes limpid as dew, the philtre is ripe for usage."

[*He rises, and stepping over to a close-fire nigh to him contemplates the stuff.*

ALCHEMIST.

'Tis an odd humour of the Duchess to

possess this love philtre.   Why, what wants she with it?   Some fine morn, a sluggish gallant will awake with love buzzing in his brain, and his blood afire.   'Tis indeed an odd humour!   Yet, ever since the Lord Marzio married, she has been strangely mannered.   And my Lord the Duke notes it not!

> [*He holds the flask up to the light. As he does so a light knock sounds against the staircase door: it opens: and the* DUCHESS *enters. A great gust of wind swirls around the tower; the rain gouts against the shuttered windows.*

DUCHESS.

Perugio?   The   philtre,   the   philtre? Quick! lest I be missed from the throng of dancers.

> [*The* ALCHEMIST *bows: he hands the flask to her.*

DUCHESS (*gladly*).

Oh, Perugio!   But—but listen?   I also lack a deadly potion, one drop of which will cause death.   I must have it now—at once.

THE ALCHEMIST (*turning to the table behind him*).

Madam! here is an extract. One small drop of this amber liquid corrupts the blood ; corroding the veins and flesh even unto death.

DUCHESS.

Give it!

ALCHEMIST (*arresting her outstretched arm*).

Not so fast! Listen. He who compounded this essence of death died by reason of the same : his unshrived soul roams eternally throughout the world : and 'tis said, that, aye the night a mortal is to die from this unsavoury draught, three times a strange tapping sounds without—the soul unshrived, striving to warn its fellow.

DUCHESS (*contemptuously*).

A tale for a winter's night with wind and robbers without ! Give it!

[*He puts the potion into the proffered hand. An evil look gathers on the beautiful face of the*

DUCHESS; *then, a baleful, triumphant smile. The winds moan
about the battlements.*

DUCHESS.

This is dearer to me than life. Only one
small drop i' the cup : and the soul has gone
from her lovelit eyes, and the pulse of her
bosom is stilled. Only one small drop !
Sir, this is sure ?

ALCHEMIST (*nodding his head*).
It has the power.

DUCHESS (*motioning to the philtre in
her left hand*).
But this philtre ! Is it proper stuff ?
[ALCHEMIST *gently removes the flask
from her left hand. He holds it
up to the light, and examines it.*

ALCHEMIST.

See. The golden colour transfuses into a
limpid clarity ; and the liquor is ripe. Ah,
madam, were I—even old and withered as I
am—were I to drink of this from your hand :

my brain and body would be drugged with the essences of Love's incitement. No peace nor rest would be mine; until Love's fruition had crowned the exalted senses!

DUCHESS (*snatching it from him*).
O Love, and Death.—To think I hold the factors of Life within the palms of these small hands!
> [*She gazes at the phials with a rapt expression upon her face: she gently shakes them.*

ALCHEMIST.
Be steady, madam—lest a drop, spilt upon your right hand, brings horrors not yet known.

DUCHESS.
Oh, I care not. But, Perugio! seal them up; lest one precious atom be lost: and, prithee, mark well the poison.
> [*She ceases. Her hands clench. A passionate gesture breaks from her. She walks rapidly up and down the room with her eyes fixed upon the floor.*

DUCHESS (*hotly*).

I see her. Marzio is with her—her, his wife. They are in the west gallery by the entrance to my tiring room—oh, I know—ensconced behind the tusser curtain, where he and I a thousand times have been. See. She clips him round the neck; and fawns upon him, worse than the meanest courtesan.—Oh, shameless! shameless! Ah! She thinks I break my heart for him. Fool!—I am here—here, conjuring your destruction.

> [*She stops suddenly, and turns round to the* ALCHEMIST, *who has been busy on the phials.*

DUCHESS (*vehemently; pointing to the death potion*).

Perugio! does it envenom? Will her veins boil with blood so foul, that her exquisite face and alluring bosom can nourish masses of loathly corruption? Will it brand her as the hideous object of hatred?

> [*She seizes him by the shoulder.*

DUCHESS (*fiercely*).
Say—it does so.

ALCHEMIST (*putting down the unclosed
phials upon the table*).
For that,—the potion needs watery dilution
to ten thousand times its bulk. So then:
one drop i' the day for a month breeds
leprosy, and many foul sores upon the
body. Nay! the afflicted is as a veritable
lazar house.

DUCHESS (*warmly*).
Rare, rare, news! God! to see her
accursed grace and beauty stink before my
eyes : the while, I have again chained
Marzio to me.—Oh, that blessed philtre of
Love ! But I must away ! You may kiss
me, Perugio—on the mouth, if you wish.
Nay, not so warmly ; but as becomes an
ancient. Fie ! fie ! you press too hard.

> [*She starts, and listens intently. The
> rushing winds whirl about the
> tower ; dashing against the un-
> curtained window a weird*

rhythm of dance music. The wafts of air cause the furnace flames to leap up: the entire room is bathed in a lurid light.

DUCHESS.

Hark to the night! How the winds roar about the towers. Hist! there are the last bars of the *Zarabanda*. I must away. But to-night—to-night—the potion for Saint Issola !

ALCHEMIST (*with deprecatory gesture*).

Madam! is there no way save by the poison ? She has no blemish in her sweet nature except all engrossing love for her lord Seigneur d'Alibert.

DUCHESS (*fiercely ; drawing herself up*).

What more? Is that not offence? Who am I, that she should have reft him from me. —I—the Duchess of Siena—the toast of a thousand feasts. I would brush a myriad Issolas from my path did they thwart me. And she ?—I shall destroy this chit—as the wanton child a fly upon the pane—part by part.   What is that?

> [*There is a sudden calm without. Two knocks ring clearly upon the battlement door.   The AL-CHEMIST starts.   Slowly he traverses the room, and flings open the door : nothing is visible. The thick darkness looms in; and the raindrops spitter upon the dusty steps.*

ALCHEMIST (*in a strained voice*).
Who is there?   Who is there?

> [*There comes no reply.   He peers out : shrinking back, he shuts the door hurriedly : then he makes the sign of the cross in a furtive manner.*

ALCHEMIST (*to himself*).
'Tis strange : no one was there.   Were there two knocks?

DUCHESS (*regarding herself in the mirror of burnished silver underneath the lamp, and arranging her mantle so as to conceal her face*).

It must have been upon the staircase door.
[*The* ALCHEMIST *opens the staircase door. He looks down the winding stairway. He shakes his head, then looks again intently.*

DUCHESS.

Why, what see you ?

ALCHEMIST (*in an odd voice*).

Seigneur d'Alibert. He is coming hither.
[*The* DUCHESS *starts. For a moment she is perturbed : then a look of great passion creeps upon her face. She clasps together her hands : a note of yearning sounds in her voice.*

DUCHESS.

Marzio—! What wants he here ? Oh, to meet him alone,—face-to-face. See, Perugio,

have the door open : I slip behind it.—So.
Now, not a word—not a word, about me.
  [MARZIO, Seigneur d'Alibert, *stum-
  bles into the room : he recovers
  his balance with an effort.*

MARZIO (*looking angrily around*).
A curse on your plaguy stairs !—my toes
are knocked out of shape ! The Duchess
here ! Never a chance on 't. I said as much
afore coming on the fool's errand, but the
rogue of a page——

ALCHEMIST (*interrupting him*).
The Duchess ?

MARZIO (*crossly*).
The same ! She has been missed some
time back. A loon of a page averred he had
noted her hurrying hither.

ALCHEMIST (*shrugging his shoulders*).
Sir, you see all. But, why seek her with
such haste ?

MARZIO.

Seek her? God's life, 'tis the Duke. He is so doting and love-crazy, that never a moment can he suffer her absence. 'Tis apparent, master alchemist, that you move but seldom from your lair among the pots and pans ;—the whole Court rings with it. Faugh! This atmosphere breathes poison. Never for a moment would she think to come here. Yet, if she did—her rare beauty would so purify the air, that, from its very sweetness, would I recognize her presence. Even now, there is a subtle savour in the place, that catches on my senses.

ALCHEMIST (*hastily*).

Ay, there are many odorous gums about.

MARZIO.

A goodly tree to distil such fragrant oozings. (*Measuredly.*) 'Tis strange : the odour catches somewhat on my memory.

> [MARZIO *sits down in the* AL-
> CHEMIST's *chair : his attitude*
> *relaxes. He closes his eyes : he*
> *breathes heavily.*

ALCHEMIST.

My Lord! a glass of strong waters?

MARZIO (*slowly*).

No, no.   'Tis nothing.

> [*He passes slowly his left hand over
> his forehead, down upon his
> eyes; then lets it fall languidly
> by his side.   He opens his eyes
> wide before him, and speaks as if
> in a trance.*

MARZIO.

It is aye the same—aye, the same.   I am
ever as a sick man dreaming dreams of his
golden summer's prime ; one, living in his
dreams ; one, dreaming throughout his life.
Oh, to encounter life red-hot at the core—or,
to feel the being reel beneath the shock of
Passion.   But, to drudge on and on; and
fetter Love, God's gift, with the iron grip of
circumstance.   Nay! 'Tis too much for any
proper man to endure.

> [*With a start* MARZIO *pauses, then
> rises and hastily paces up and
> down the room.*

ALCHEMIST.

My Lord,—what ails you ?
[*The* DUCHESS *drops her pomander
box.* MARZIO *stops.*

ALCHEMIST.

A pestle, my Lord, a pestle fallen from its
place. What ails you ?

MARZIO (*in an outburst*).

Ails me—what ails me, you ask ? Sir,
what knowledge have you of the flesh ?
What drug can dull the keen edge of ever
poignant memory, or cause the unforgetful
to forget. Her face to-night—her flower-
like face with its dark passionate eyes set
hotly upon mine : her tender lips, like opening buds upon her ruddy mouth : her grace ;
her beauty. And that peddling dotard, the
Duke, by her side at the feast ;—leering upon
her ;—stealing his lean arm about her, until he
had embraced her, even before our sight.
—'Tis hell itself to think on't :—and she once
mine ! Oh, fool, fool,—to enrich honour at
the expense of self.
[*He flings himself into the chair ; his*

*throbbing head upon the palms
of his hands. The* ALCHEMIST
*approaches, and lays his hand
upon* MARZIO. *The* DUCHESS
*makes an uncertain movement
towards them.* MARZIO *looks
up before him : she retires again.*

ALCHEMIST.
My Lord, be calm !

MARZIO (*looking up*).
Calm !—Be calm—you said. Shall the fire
cease its heat ? or the sea, its motion ?—Then,
indeed, passion shall cease to madden men.
Ay, passion—nought, but brute passion.
Tush ! be silent; and save your wind. Prate
to me of honour, who never knew what
womanly honour is, until, alas, too late for
valuation ! who only appraised her purity
from impure motives ! Ah, Issola ! Have I
not fought for purity and probity of heart.
For you, have I not striven a thousand times
against this blind passion, that consumes
me ; against this glamour, still thrown in
the mere flicker of a woman's eyes. Ah,

Issola, you can ne'er even imagine the case.
(*Springs up.*) Sir! is there no magic, no
potion, that can drive this obsession from me.
Drug me—spell me : but free me from this
hidden witchery of the flesh. (*Recalls
himself.*) Pshaw! how I screed like a madman. So, sir, I can say the Duchess is not
here?

> [MARZIO *steps towards the door. His
> foot knocks against the pomander
> box, driving it away. He stops
> and stares at it—his finger
> pointed towards it. As the
> ALCHEMIST rushes forward to
> pick it up the DUCHESS steps
> out from behind the door—her
> face ghastly pale. She stretches
> out her arms towards* MARZIO :
> *with a little inarticulate cry, she
> swoons against the door, which
> shuts with a metallic clang.*

ALCHEMIST.

Madam! Madam!

> [MARZIO *springs forward. Suddenly
> he halts; a look of amazement*

Q

*and consternation flashes upon
his face. The* DUCHESS *opens
her eyes.*

MARZIO (*bowing low*).
The Duchess !

DUCHESS (*with an effort recovering herself*).
Yes, the Duchess.   Sir, you are searching
for me?

MARZIO (*bowing*).
The Duke demands your presence.

DUCHESS.
Demands! God, every touch of his stings
me like an asp ! And you—I caught your
eye to-night, as he kissed me on the cheek.
Marzio, come back to me—come back to
me.

ALCHEMIST (*expostulating, puts his hand upon
her arm*).
Madam, the Duke !
[*She takes no heed but advances*

towards MARZIO, *who steps
back until he is nigh to the
hanging lamp.*

ALCHEMIST (*more intensely*).
Madam, you are the Duchess !

DUCHESS.

Oh, I am the Duchess : and what of
that ? Can I not love ? The merest scullion
maid can choose her mate : but I—born to a
loveless marriage, bound to a wooden stock
called a husband—am I not flesh and blood?
Can I too not love and hate ? I am the
Duchess: and I am a woman.

[MARZIO *opens his lips, then shuts
them determinedly. A pained
expression grows upon his face :
suddenly his eyes close, his shoulders fall. The* DUCHESS *looks at
him with a passionate-lit glance,
then swiftly approaches him.*

DUCHESS (*softly*).
Marzio ?

MARZIO (*striving to recall himself; looking up at her*).
Madam, the Duke desires your presence.
[*The* DUCHESS *makes an angry gesture: she turns upon her heel, and walks towards the staircase door. Of a sudden, she comes back to him: a curious look grows upon her lovely face, her eyes glow with a strange light.*

ALCHEMIST (*intercepting her*).
Madam, be mistress of yourself! Leave him.
[*But the* DUCHESS *pays no heed. She advances so near* MARZIO *that her breasts touch his shoulder, her breath moves his wavy hair. She fixes her great eyes intensely upon his face: half clinging upon him, she twines her fingers about his right hand.*

DUCHESS (*slowly, passionately*).
Marzio! Not one word for me ?—not one.
[*He trembles: gives way: throwing*

The Potion.

*himself at her feet, he casts his
arms about her, and kisses hotly
the cloth of her gown.*

MARZIO.

Viola. Viola.
*[But in an instant he throws himself
from her, and springs up.*

MARZIO *(wildly).*
No! no! Save me from myself! Help
me, oh God! God! Hear me. *(Speaking
with great effort.)* Go. Your husband awaits
you.

> *[He indicates the door to the* DUCHESS,
> *who is looking at him with im-
> movable eyes. Yet of a sudden
> he casts down his sight from her
> all-devouring gaze; the out-
> stretched arm falls by his side.
> A great look of triumph flashes
> over her face, and is gone.*

> *The* ALCHEMIST *is stepping
> between them, when suddenly he
> falls back with a motion of
> terror, as a tapping upon a*

*door reverberates loudly through
the stillness. A mighty clap of
wind clamours about the tower.*

ALCHEMIST (*turning towards the staircase door ;
in awestruck voice*).

Again! It is the warning. But yet ;—the
third time.—The third time.

[*He withdraws from the laboratory.
Neither* MARZIO *nor the* DUCH-
ESS *stirs ; nor do they hear the*
ALCHEMIST'S *footsteps sound
loudly on the stairway, then die
away as he recedes. Suddenly
the* DUCHESS *advances swiftly
to* MARZIO'S *side, and closes
upon him.*

DUCHESS (*impetuously*).

Marzio! what need of foolish scruples?
Have we not loved and suffered: let us
love again. Love is God's gift ; it knows
no control, nor abatement from that false
notion called honour : for, Love is Nature's
eternal Law of sex and sex ; the ordinance

that rules the universe. Marzio, my Marzio,
be blind no longer to the truth. We two
loved, and parted. We two have striven
to live apart. Yet in vain. For, as surely
as the tide meets the main in its ceaseless
ebb and flow, so we meet again, again; and
yet again. Be wise. Fate has decreed it.
Marzio! speak to me.

> [MARZIO *looks at her for an instant.*
> *Mastering himself, he turns*
> *away his gaze. He moves*
> *somewhat from her.*

MARZIO (*thickly*).

Viola! you speak, what I ne'er thought
to have heard again from you. Ever for the
past months your words have rung in my
ears:—"'Tis best you marry her: and we
part." You said so with mocking laughter
in your voice: and the very devils in Hell
grinned at the news. Hush! Nay, I never
spoke so cruelly to you. Have you for-
gotten so soon: never shall I. The words
scorched deep into my brain as you uttered
them that night we stood upon the terrace,
within the shadow of the cypress tree. My

hands were on your shoulders—my lips upon
your cheek (I thought on that, when he
kissed you this evening at the board). I was
wild ; torn with passionate desire, with doubts
and fears : but you—you grew so calm, and
cold, and saintly—just like one of sculptor
Baldarasso's little angels in the chapel. I remember well—you stirred apart and nipped
a firefly between your fingers. " 'Tis best
you marry her : and we part " said you ; and
moved my hot hands from off your bosom.
The very moonbeam, flitting upon your face,
shared in your disdain, and concealed your
eyes and crimson mouth in the darkness——

DUCHESS (*interrupting him*).
Marzio ! Marzio ! say no more ! I was
mad with the bitter jealousy of an unheeded
woman——

MARZIO (*without attention to her*).
So calm and saintly you were, that I deemed
cold reason had quenched Love's potency ;—
that no longer were you my beloved, but
Viola, Duchess of Siena, recalling me to my

The Potion. 233

duty towards the State and her; the paramount
lady of the land. So, as the Duke elected,
I wooed Issola, my pure-souled Issola. Yet,
day and night, I see nothing, but one woman's
face—hear nothing, but one woman's voice
ringing in my ears.

> [*He stops, then strides to her and
> grips her by the arm. Both
> stand underneath the lamp. In
> a near corner, from out some
> alembic, wavering circles of
> vapour float upwards to the
> stone ceiling, and, gathering,
> slowly creep along the dusty
> rubble work like a tangled cloud-
> let. Without, the wind has
> fallen, the rain is a mere
> drizzle, the music of the dancers
> sounds loudly, and the noise of
> the changing guards. Within,
> all is silence save the occa-
> sional crackle of the charcoal.*

MARZIO (*hotly*).
If I stand again with you in the shadow of
that tree. Would you kiss me back ? Would

you reject me, if I sued ? Speak. (*Flings her arm away.*) Bah ! I think the old madness lasts; but, not the pain, not the pain, of your disdain.

> [*He turns from her, and walks quickly up and down the dim place.*

DUCHESS (*flinging out her arms to him*).
Marzio ! I was not myself. I was crazed with an evil, jealous imagination. To have you look upon another woman was as a slash across my heart. I know men are wantons : and, that you should have dared to fling one glance or thought elsewhere, than to me, maddened me as only jealous love can madden. I was wrong, Marzio. I was quite wrong.

> [MARZIO *stops short in his pacing to and fro : he gives vent to a bitter, short laugh.*

MARZIO (*indignantly, vehemently*).
I look on another woman ! There is but one woman in the world.—The world rings with her name :—Viola, Viola. I throw looks and thoughts at other women! Never an

hour passes, but you slip into my mind un-
awares, and turn foul to fair, darkness to
light. Never a night, but my heart cries
for you ; and, dreaming, I awake to hear my
call of " Viola " echoing in the air. I— !
God's life ! and what of the sweet favours,
and smiles, thrown to every cringing courtier.
This one to kiss your hand, because he plucks
a lily from the moat and has wet his toes
at the marge—that one to encircle your
dainty foot and ankle as you swing into the
saddle.

[With a sudden gesture he advances
upon her.

MARZIO (*hotly ; recklessly*).
You—you arraign me—you, who claim
my service—body, mind, and——

DUCHESS (*interrupting him with a triumphant*
cry ; flinging her arms about him).
—And love.

[Involuntarily their lips meet. Again
the night has grown stormy :
the wind and rain lash against
the tower : but, above the tempest

*sound the strange rhythms of
the Zarabanda, waxing and
waning as the wind changes.*

MARZIO (*controlling himself with an
effort ; disengaging her*).
No! you must not.   Go to the Duke.

DUCHESS (*positively*).
Beloved!   Love knows nought except his
own calls.
[*She kisses him again ; and clings
tenderly upon him.   MARZIO
puts her a little from him.*

MARZIO.
Nay, not so!   It is your duty.   We two
have dreamed life's sweetest dream.   (Oh,
once more, to dream such a dream: then
die.)   Hush!   hear me.   Love is the all-in-
all of Life;   but Life, not of Love.   There
are demands and duties, tasks and obligations,
higher and holier than Love's.

DUCHESS (*falling from him*).
Why !   what mean you ?

MARZIO.

You have the Duke; the State: I—Issola; and my birthright of manhood. Our distinct duties are demanded of us. Fate has written it so.

DUCHESS (*warmly*).

'Twas Fate threw us together. We cannot part: for 'twixt man and woman Love and Fate are one.

MARZIO (*sadly; shaking his head*).

You err: 'twas Passion, not Love, that threw us together; and Passion is but a base growth. Love, that knows not the beloved from her body, nor her body from herself: that is Fate.

> [*The* DUCHESS *rests her head for a moment on his shoulder: she kisses the lace collar of his doublet: then stares before her.* MARZIO *strokes her dark tresses. He takes her hand, and presses his lips upon the fragrant palm.*

MARZIO.

Madam! we will hurry to the Duke. He will indeed be uneasy.

DUCHESS (*with a swift motion removes herself; she puts a hand upon her throbbing forehead*).
I know not what this means. Oh, how my head does ache !

> [*She wavers, then falls backwards—* MARZIO *catches her. With a sigh, she puts her arms round his neck, her head upon his shoulder.*

DUCHESS (*reproachfully*).
Marzio, your words are cruel : they cut me to the heart. Let us love, while love we may.

MARZIO (*his eyes closed; his voice thick with suppressed emotion*).
They are cruel : me, also, they cut to the heart. But the truth must be told. Viola, each has but pandered to the other's passions : even our surrender was the fruition of selfish, inborn desire. Where is no abnegation of self—body, mind, and soul—is no love. Passion was our portion—brute passion.

The Potion. 239

[For a second both are still: she look-
ing straight before her at his
strained face. Suddenly she
throws herself from his arms,
and seems as if striving to re-
call herself. She brushes the
hair back from her forehead
and temples : she is agitated
strangely.

DUCHESS.

Ah, ah ! (*Stranglingly in her throat; then*
fiercely.) Your arms, sir, keep them for your
Issola—your Saint Issola. (*She steps back, and*
looks contemptuously at him.) Tied to her
girdle strings! Seigneur d'Alibert—a woman's
pap-child! Love! what knows your saint of
Love? Can she drench the soul with such
ecstasy that it swoonds beneath its load ? Can
she enwrap the senses, and make the unreal
real—this common earth into Heaven's self?
Oh, man ! am I mad ? Do I live ? Or is all
this one horrid mockery of make-believe? Oh,
to think I have loved such an ignoble creature. To think, that for you I risked fair
fame and fortune, threw honour to the winds

and made chastity a by-date in my calendar.
Vile wretch. I—a Duchess—to sue at your
feet ; to proffer this matchless face and
figure, these tender arms and hands, a sacrifice
to you.—Oh, the shame will kill me.   Yes,
sir! tell the Duke I come.

> [*The* DUCHESS *points significantly to
> the door.* MARZIO *staggers
> towards it like a giddy person :
> he half turns, and, speaking
> with difficulty, totters upon his
> feet.*

MARZIO.

Madam ! Loved I not Honour now—so
would I love you the less. (*Turns to the door.*)
How she hates me—how she hates me.

> [*Suddenly he puts his hands to his side.*

MARZIO.

'Tis as a hand gripped my heart.   My
head swims.   I—I——

> [*He reels backwards into the chair
> beneath the flickering lamp : to
> his right is the table, whereon are*

the potion and philtre. The
Duchess *springs forward to*
him.

Duchess (*urgently anxious*).
Marzio ! I did not mean what I said.
Speak to me—speak to me !
[*She kneels by his side: her voice is*
full of passionate entreaty.

Duchess.
It was my head—not my heart—that
prompted my cruel words. I—I love you
yet, Marzio.
[*She leans her head affectionately*
against him; her arms seek
round him. Marzio's *head is*
thrown back: his breath comes
in pants : his voice is thick and
suffocated.

Marzio.
I know not, what I do, or say. It is hard
to do the right—to do the right, and not sin.
[*He passes his hand over his brows ;*
R

and gives vent to an in-articulate moan. The DUCHESS peers intently at him. A sudden thought flashes into her head : a joyous, triumphant look gathers upon her face. She glances around for the philtre, and, observing it, arises to her feet ; yet fronting the table so as to conceal the phials, she puts out her right hand behind her and seizes a phial. Still considering him with eyes close-set, with that look of increasing triumph and love deepening upon her beautiful face, she pours out the liquid.

DUCHESS (*softly, persuasively*).
Marzio, drink this cordial : and we will hurry to the Duke.
[*She puts the goblet into his hand. Like a man in a dream he drinks. For an instant, he holds the goblet in his trembling hand, then, with a shrill cry, flings it from him.*

The Potion. 243

MARZIO (*rising up; his voice choked*).
Ah—ah—(*Mightily.*) Viola. Viola.
[*So, crying aloud her name, he falls
dead at her feet. The* DUCHESS
*screams: she flings her hands
upon her face.*

DUCHESS.
The poison !—the poison !
[*She sways heavily above her lover's
corpse. The tempest rages without: yet, even above the screaming
of the wind, two raps sound
without. With a howl, the
wind bursts open the battlement
door: the rain beats in; the
drops hiss as they fall upon the
hot alembics and furnaces: from
the lower reach of the castle ring
the strange cadences of the
Zarabanda; weirdly rising and
falling upon the eddying wind.
The* DUCHESS *starts: she stares
fixedly beyond the open door, out
into the black raging night. Suddenly, she screams with terror.*

DUCHESS (*incoherently*).
What is that shadow? There. There.
Coming near: and nearer. It is—it is—
No, God. God—not yet. No, Death,—not
yet, not yet.   Ah—(*screams*). Marzio.
Marzio.

> [*So, screaming aloud his name, she
> falls dead across his body. Yet,
> ever the Zarabanda sounds on.*

Lammastide, 1897.

FINIS.

www.ingramcontent.com/pod-product-compliance
Lightning Source LLC
Chambersburg PA
CBHW030807020726

47499CB00006B/1807